DEAD LOST

JACK ZOMBIE #6

FLINT MAXWELL

Copyright © 2018 by Flint Maxwell

Cover Design © 2018 by Carmen Rodriguez

All rights reserved. No portion of this book may be reproduced in any form without permission from the publisher, except as permitted by U.S. copyright law. For permissions email: fm@flintmaxwell.com

This is a work of fiction. Names, characters, places, and incidents either are the products of the author's imagination or are used fictitiously. Any resemblance to actual persons, living or dead, businesses, companies, events, or locales is entirely coincidental.

The author greatly appreciates you taking the time to read his work.

This one is for all of the Flint-Stones out there

Let's not forget that freedom is more powerful than fear.

— Barack Obama

1

Wrong.

Staring the dead man in his face, that is what I'm thinking.

Wrong.

He comes toward me on the dark road. I stand somewhere near the faded yellow line, barely visible this night.

I hold a sword in my hand, a weapon I've picked up from one of those weird, novelty medieval shops. A long broadsword you might see in an epic fantasy movie. Well, when they were still making movies, that is. I don't think one has been made for close to fifteen years. I don't think one will ever be made again.

The blade is easy enough to wield, especially for

a schmuck like me who's not very practiced in the art of swordplay.

The zombie makes these noises, this low growling in his throat. I can't tell if his teeth are rotten from chewing all that dead flesh or from chewing a bunch of tobacco.

Doesn't matter.

He's close enough for me to smell him.

I take a big whiff—mostly involuntary.

After all these years around zombies, I'm still not used to that awful smell of decay and bile and death. It's easier to stomach, I guess, but not one of my favorite scents, that's for sure. It's easily the worst part of being on the road. Aside from the loneliness.

I swing down hard.

Lucky for me, though, the sword is sharp and it cleaves through the zombie's head like a hot knife through butter.

Brains and a mist of blood spray toward me. I don't even flinch. I've been covered in so much zombie gunk, it's a permanent part of my wardrobe now.

The dead guy's mouth opens in a confused gape. Think about a fish out of water, rubbery lips moving for that sweet water-oxygen or whatever the fuck it is that fishes survive on.

Dead Lost

Somewhere beneath my thick and graying beard, a smile spreads on my face. It's times like now that I wish I'd kept count of how many of these dead or *undead* bastards I've put back into the ground. With the fun—fun, now that I look back on it—I've had with Molotov cocktails and grenades, that number is sky-high, no doubt.

The zombie falls forward, two cleaved sides of his head sliding down my blade. I'm going to have to clean it again. With his eyes so far apart, he kind of *does* remind me of a fish. He falls forward. Usually, as per our seemingly arbitrary pop culture rules, killing the brain kills the monster, but sometimes, a particular asshole-ish zombie will twitch or moan before it crosses over to the afterlife. I've grown to expect this.

What I don't expect is for this asshole to swipe at me with hands that are much too strong for a dead zombie. He latches on to my shirt collar and pulls it down beneath where my cloak is tied. Sure, that's all good fun, and I wouldn't mind much under normal circumstances, but he grabs my necklace along with my collar.

Dead weight is heavy weight, and I can't stop it from pulling the small silver chain from my neck. It makes this *clink* that carries in the silent surrounding forest. For a long moment, I think it's the actual sound of my heart breaking.

This chain and the pendant attached to it is special. More special than I thought anything in my life would be to me right now.

The chain pops and I feel it slither off my neck. When it's completely gone, it's like I'm missing a talisman, my only form of protection in this fucked-up world.

Of course the zombie's head is leaking black, gooey brains and the necklace is lost in all this. I have one pair of gloves, leather, real durable, real nice. It's not worth it to get them all ruined and *gummy*.

I'll have to dig through the gore with my bare-fucking-hands. Awesome.

Looking at the zombie's oozing head, I think of what Humpty Dumpty might have really looked like when he fell off of the wall and busted himself into a bunch of pieces. I think of a smashed, infected egg, black yolk, and a rotten embryo running out of it.

I *really* don't want to have to dig through this.

But I know I will.

For the little piece of my dead wife and son I have left, I will do anything.

2

AFTER DIGGING THROUGH THE MESS, NOT EVEN gagging once—shit, I've seen it all...brains, guts, and even zombies hung up by their spinal cords—I walk onward.

A lot has changed since the last time you've heard from me. Nearly fifteen years have passed.

For those of you who don't know me well, my legal name is Jack Jupiter. God, it's weird to think of myself as Jack Jupiter again. It's been over two years since someone has called me that.

The world, as you might have guessed or known, has ended. A disease, a plague, an Armageddon, whatever the hell you want to call it, has swept across our globe. It started fifteen or sixteen years ago just outside of my hometown, Woodhaven

Ohio. A place that has long since burned down. A place I do not miss in the slightest.

I've traveled the United States with my family (a blood relative and a few adopted members) in pursuit of a cure and survival. I've failed. Eventually, I found a safe place in San Francisco called Haven. I helped keep it safe. I settled down, got married, and started a family. I don't know what I was thinking. In hindsight, it does not seem possible to have a family when the dead walk and hunt us like animals. But I figured I'd survived this long, how much harder could it be to keep my family alive? How much longer could I keep us together?

Thirteen years, that's how long.

That was when Haven was attacked, when a group of demented killers calling themselves the District stormed our gates.

We'd been living in peace for so long we never expected that. We were blinded by our own hubris. My wife Darlene's throat was slit right in front of my son and I. Then my son was shot in the back of the head. Herb Jr. was only thirteen when the one-eyed man pulled the trigger at point blank range. My own son's blood dotted my face.

The one-eyed man has left me alive. He wanted me to live with this, wanted me to suffer.

Big mistake. He should've killed me.

For six months after their deaths, I was in a haze. I drank until I blacked out every night, drank with the intent of killing myself because I was too cowardly to do it any other way—like bite down on a barrel and pull the trigger or dive headlong into a pit of the squirming, starving zombies.

Then something clicked. I realized I didn't have to sit around feeling sad for myself. Of course, I miss Darlene and Herb Jr. more than anything and there's times—usually in the dead of night when all is quiet and my mind runs a million miles an hour—where I don't think I can keep being strong, but I know I have to. I could go out there and find that one-eyed man. I could take down his brainwashed followers, the District. I could do it all because I'm Jack Jupiter.

And that's exactly what I'm going to do.

There is something else, too, something else keeping me going.

I scoured the destroyed remains of Haven for nearly a week as I looked for my brother Norman, and my apocalypse-adopted sister Abby. I did not find their bodies. Part of me thought they might've been completely devoured by the zombies who'd been attracted to the flames and sounds of gunfire, and that still could be the case, but I don't think so.

Deep down in my heart, I know they are somewhere out there. They are survivors, and they weren't there when the other leaders of Haven and I were put on trial in front of the rest of the survivors, when Darlene and my son were taken from me.

Yes, I think they're out there. Where, though? I have no idea. Currently, that is not my greatest concern. My greatest concern is revenge. It is all that fuels me, all that keeps me putting one foot in front of the other.

The sun is coming up by the time I see the distant outpost. I take a map out of my important pocket, a map I took off of a man who tried to rob me on the road. One look at myself and I can understand why he had thought I was an easy target. One look at the caved-in face of this particular road bandit, and you'd understand why it is not wise to mess with me. Anyway, the map this man had was a crude rendering of the surrounding Midwestern states. I am somewhere outside of what used to be Chicago, about fifty or so miles. Chicago was where Darlene and I used to live. Then my mother died and I was brought back to Ohio for her funeral, and then, of course, everything spiraled out of control and fifteen years later, here I am.

On this map, there are places crossed out in dark

permanent marker. Take Springfield for example. Scribbled over it, scrawled by a hand that hadn't spent much time writing or learning their alphabet, is EMPIRE PARK, and nearby are other smaller places with the same crooked letters written over their proper name.

I am near Aurora. This place is called Freeland now. This is the distant outpost I see, I'm guessing. I think about avoiding it. It seems most of these outposts are crawling with men and women from the District. Some of them have recognized me, but they never lived to tell anyone about it.

I am tired, and I do not wish to sleep on the hard ground this early morning. Because I have recently seen and killed a zombie, I am on edge. So I continue walking up this road. As I get closer to the outpost, I see the looming walls built of scrap metal and stacked junk cars. I see two snipers' nest and wonder if the men and women in them have their sights currently trained on me.

I weave in and out of blockades. From behind the walls, a column of smoke rises. The air is sweet with the smell of cook-fires, roasting meat. Hardly any smell of disease and death here. Freeland is looking more and more like a good place to hunker down for the day.

I know the risks, but my exhaustion and fear are too much to bear.

As I come upon the gates, a light shines on me. I wear the hood of my cloak up, and my right hand is inside my important pocket, fingering the locket, thinking of Darlene and Junior. My son's name was Herbert Junior, as I've said earlier; he was named after one of the many people dear to my heart that I'd lost on my journey to San Francisco and Haven, but Herbert Junior wasn't too fond of his name. This change came around the time he started school. He said he didn't like the name, but we knew the truth. His classmates made fun of him. I get it, I really do. I know all about getting made fun of. The name Freddy Huber comes to mind. He was my mortal enemy in high school and, *un*surprisingly, still was when I came back to bury my mother a decade later.

"State your business," a gruff voice says from behind the light. I pull my hand out of my pocket and hold both of them up to show I'm not dangerous. The truth is, if you've survived this long in zombie-land, then you're definitely dangerous. You'd have to be a dummy to not know that.

"Just looking for a place to stay for the day," I say.

The guard looks at me like I'm stupid. It makes me want to punch him in the face. If he wasn't up in that tower, I probably would. Then again, that might be a bad idea. I really *could* use a bed right now. According to the road bandit's map, the next town not ravaged by zombies is a few miles away. If I were in a car, I'd flip these guards in their watchtowers the finger and be on my way. Alas, I am not. I'm walking.

The most recent car I had...well, that didn't end in my favor. Let's just say driving an old Ford Focus through a sea of zombies is not the brightest idea I've ever had. Get enough blood and guts gunked up in the grille and mechanical failures are bound to happen.

"What's your name?"

"Jack."

"Well, Jack, you have to pay the toll to get in," the gruff voice says, and judging by the way he speaks, I think that's total bullshit.

"Thought this place was called Freeland," I say and point to the sign. "Or can't you read?"

The light clicks off. My eyes take a moment to adjust, but when they do I see I'm not dealing with the kind of guy who can take jokes. I can also tell this guy isn't with the District. You can see the crazy in District peoples' eyes. Can practically smell it on them, too. Seeing how this guy isn't one of my mortal enemies, it's safe to say that I'd rather save my energy and not knock his teeth in.

Besides, he currently has an assault rifle pointed down on me. I feel no fear. I've had many guns aimed in my face. Hell, I've even been shot once or twice. Got the scars to prove it.

"What's your price?" I ask, sighing.

"What do you got?"

I reach into my pocket and feel around. I pull out a handful of batteries. "Got double and triple A's, got nine-volts, lithium ion, Energizer, Duracell, you name it."

"Give me four double A's," the guard says, "then I'll let you in."

In my hand, I only have two double A's, and that's all I've got. I hold up a finger, saying I need more time.

"No funny business," the other guard says. "We'll shoot you." The quiver in his voice tells me he won't. Can never be too sure. I've been surprised before.

I dig in a different pocket. My hands are fast. I drop the batteries back in the good pocket and pull out four duds I kept for exactly this purpose. People love their fucking batteries in the apocalypse, and these are the batteries I used in an old Walkman. Played *Hot Rocks* by the Stones until the batteries practically coughed and Mick Jagger's voice faded to a dull whine. So yeah, they're duds, but this asshole all high and mighty on his watchtower with his assault rifle doesn't know that.

I hold them in my palm.

"Throw them up," he says, obviously meaning one at a time. I let all four go at once. He catches one, maybe two, and the rest make the sound of gunshots carrying across the empty road behind me as they bang off the wood planks of the sniper's nest.

"There's your toll. Let me in," I say.

The gruff voiced guard is too busy trying to find the other two batteries so I glare at his pal across from him. The guard practically melts at my death stare. I don't often look at my reflection these days, no reason to really, but the last time I did, which was a couple days ago, I almost spooked myself. I was kneeling down over a stream, about to fill up my canteen when I saw my face as clear as day in the slow running water. My eyes are sunken into my head and there's blue-purple rings beneath them that make me look like quite the walking corpse myself. My beard is much too long and unruly. Same goes for my hair, which is long enough that it lays flat and out of my face, easy to slick back. There's gray in both my hair and beard. Wrinkles around my eyes from squinting so much. If you shaved my beard, you might see wrinkles around my mouth, too. Those are from laughing. When Darlene and Junior were still around, when Haven was working like a well-oiled machine and Norm and Tim and Abby and Carmen and Eve were heading the council with me, it was almost like the world was normal. We laughed a lot in those days. I don't laugh much now, not anymore. They're all gone, and here I am, paying my way into an apocalyptic town with batteries. Amazing how life can change so drastically, so fast.

So my features are enough to spook this guard into opening the gates. He takes a handle in his hand and starts cranking it fast. Tires spin up there, rubber grinding against rubber, metal screeches and the gate opens slowly, exposing the sleepy town within.

No people are out on the streets. I don't blame them, the sun is barely up. I see an old brick building that looks like it might've been a convenience store many moons ago, a post office, the faded USPS logo a blast from the past, a gas station, a bank that has been converted into an armory. I walk through the threshold of the opening.

"First sign of funny business," the gruff voiced

guard says to me, "and I shoot your face off. We mean it."

Very hospitable, I think as I ignore him.

I travel the dusty road, taking it all in. It's not much; Haven looked a thousand times better than this place. But it's something. It's a slice of civilization, what I've been longing for ever since the downfall of the world came and went. They called it *The End* when it happened. Entire countries collapsed in the blink of an eye. The disease spread so fast—*Like a raging wildfire,* an old acquaintance of mine named Pat Huber once told me—that humanity truly had no hope. Fifteen years later, and I still don't know why I was among one of the few humans who weren't affected by the disease or why the zombies haven't rotten into piles of dust. Whatever disease they cooked up in the Leering lab was really potent.

We didn't know much about it when it happened—and I'm not trying to be clandestine here. I'm not trying to say I was apart of some secret government organization that was studying the disease or anything like that, though I *did* have a pretty gnarly shootout with said government organization. They are called Central—*were* called Central. I didn't leave any alive.

Anyway, I was a writer, not a soldier or a cop or some macho douchebag you usually see in zombie movies. I wrote horror novels, but my bread and butter were zombie books. I don't write anymore. At least not physically. I do, however, make up stuff in my head all the time, to pass the time. Mostly a fictionalized version of what happened to Haven, an alternate ending, if you're into DVD extras, an ending where the District never storm Haven's gates and take everything from me, an ending where Darlene, Junior, and I live happily ever after, where Norm and Tim and Abby and her husband Mike and Darlene's sister Carmen and her mom Eve do the same.

Back to the disease. Like I said, we didn't know much about it when it first broke out. Over the years, I discovered more. There was a woman who came to Haven who had been affiliated with the US government. She worked in the CDC. They were tasked with finding a cure after Central failed to weaponize it. The disease affected, by their estimates, nearly half of the world's population. What she meant by *affected* was that the disease killed them and brought them back as undead nightmares. The other fifty percent of the world's population, especially in the beginning, were caught off guard. The disease is easily spread through a zombie bite.

So this other half of the population had been unprepared as most of us undoubtedly always are. They were bitten by loved ones on their deathbeds, they were attacked while looting grocery stores and pharmacies, they were gunned down by the military by accident, by bombs in larger US cities and foreign countries.

But who knows if that woman was telling the truth? I don't even remember her name.

All I know for sure is that the outbreak originated near my hometown of Woodhaven at the Leering Research Facility and that I'm still here while seventy to eighty percent of the population is probably either dead or a zombie.

So I got a lot of shit going against me, but that's nothing new.

Jack Jupiter knows adversity. Like I've said, I've seen it all, taken down warlords, saved the fucking world.

Still walking, I turn a corner and what I see causes me to stumble to a stop. Well, at least I *thought* I'd seen it all.

3

It's not a zombie or the one-eyed man—as much as I wish it were him. It's never that easy.

It's actually a downed plane. One of those big military types. I've only ever seen one in the movies, but they're bigger in real life than they are on the big screen. This one is a weather-faded green and big enough to haul a couple tanks. Probably. I really don't know. Crumbled brick and rubble gather at the plane's nose. It crashed into this poor building. I wonder how many people died during the incident. Too many, I'm sure.

What's weird about all of this—besides the fact that the crash is still here—is that the plane isn't some abandoned accordion of metal. It looks lived in.

To confirm my hypothesis, a group of men stumble out of a makeshift door just under the broken wing. Coincidentally, the piece of metal that was the wing is now a ramp and these guys nearly fall over the railing. They're laughing and patting each other on the back. I watch from about twenty feet away. I have my cloak on, hood still up, and I'm in the shadows. Even if I was stark naked and the sun was beating down on me, I don't think these men would notice.

They're drunk off their asses. Spent the whole night hammering down flat beer and old whiskey. I envy the sense of camaraderie and togetherness these men share. It's something I once had with Norm and Abby, and, of course, my wife.

Now they're off the ramp and heading toward a building at the end of the street. It's a three story brick place with a swinging sign over the door. I can't read it. My eyes aren't as good as they used to be.

Although it doesn't take someone with perfect sight to realize that's the town motel. A place for weary travelers and warlords.

I look back to the downed plane. I now notice the sign in one of the windows. It reads: THE JET in a cursive letters, a pub, the local watering hole.

Funny how society tries to hold onto the things of the past.

Then part of me is thinking, *Well Jack, that's exactly what you're doing...*

I try to ignore that part of myself.

I could really use a drink, though. Places like that always accept batteries and the other types of useful trinkets I keep in my pockets. I can go in there and find out about this place, maybe even find out about the District this far east. Haven't heard of them in a while. People out here either don't bend their knees to crazy warlords or they're just too stupid to care.

At least, I hope.

I cross the quiet street and head up the ramp, into the corpse of an military airplane.

4

Batwing doors. It's like an old west saloon. As I push them open and the current of upbeat piano music runs over me, I resist the urge to throw my cloak back to reveal the pistol on my hip and spit tobacco into a brass spittoon with a resounding *ding*. Yeah...I've seen way too many Westerns.

Couple things wrong with that scenario anyway. First, I like to keep the pistol on my hip a surprise. It's a last resort, if you will. When you're trekking through miles of zombie country, the last thing you want to do is draw more of the bastards toward you by pulling the trigger of your hand cannon.

Lessons learned in the wasteland.

Inside the bar, the atmosphere isn't as sleepy as

the town, but it's not very lively, either. I'm not surprised to see they've extended the interior of the plane, knocked out a back wall and built around it. Other than the metal walls and floor, this place is quite the standard Western saloon. In Illinois, I might add.

There's a pretty bartender behind the counter. She's got short dark hair and sharp cheekbones. Her blue eyes glow in the low light. She smiles at me. I wonder if she works for tips and just what the heck people tip her with. I smile back and she looks away as soon as I do it. It's been too long since I've smiled at another human being. Zombies don't give a shit whether my smile is as idiotic as it feels on my face. Apparently pretty bartenders do.

I survey the room.

Always do that. Weed out any threats.

The place is mostly dead, though, like the world. In the back right corner a couple of men sip from mugs with heavy eyes. Even the piano player to my left hits the keys with as much force as a ghost. At the bar is a man who has not starved. His girth causes the stool beneath his massive behind to creak and groan with the slightest movements. He's the liveliest patron in here, and that's also really not saying much. The bartender pours another beer into this guy's mug. It doesn't froth, as flat as ever. The man gulps it down regardless. My experience with beer is, after you start feeling a buzz, your taste buds go *'Aw, screw it!'* and you can down as much beer as possible without noticing that bitter taste .

I walk up to the bar and take a stool three spaces down from the guy. A couple signs hum behind the bartender, an old neon Bud Light and a Heineken. The Bud Light is the more vibrant of the two with its red, white, and blue—America's beer, right?

"What'll you have?" the bartender asks. She speaks in a cutesy voice I know is not the voice she uses outside of work.

"What do you got?"

"Name it."

I'm not much of a drinker. As I've said, after Darlene and Junior died, I drank more than any man who still has a functioning liver should. I've had enough.

I lean over the bar and peer down. It is a sound that has drawn my attention, the hum of a refrigerator. It's a sound I haven't heard since Haven. Our budding community had running electricity, running water, central air and heat in some of the compounds. We were spreading, too. It was the council's goal to bring San Francisco closer and closer to what it once was with every generation. We had something good. *I* had something good.

The sadness strikes me hard, and I feel my eyes filling with tears. I look down at the floor, bringing the back of my hand up to swipe at them. Little moisture. Damn it, keep it together, Jack.

I thought I've gotten better at that—putting it to the back of my mind. It just never stays there. Comes sliding up behind you, like a legless zombie.

"You looking at the fridge?" the bartender asks, snapping me out of whatever haze I'm currently in. Suddenly, I'm self-conscious. She's close to me, too close. It's been a long while since I've been this close to a woman, and she smells nice, like perfume and mouthwash. I can't imagine what I smell like. I've been on the road for two years, but it's been about a week since I've slept under a roof or had a shower. Sure, I rinse off whenever I find a body of water, but that's not enough to get rid of the funk clinging to me.

"Yeah, I am. You have any old cans of Coca-Cola in there. I'm willing to pay." Been fifteen years since the Coke factory's made a fresh batch, but that doesn't bother me. When you live off of old cheese and stale crackers, a flat Coca-Cola is a treat.

The bartender smirks. "Not much of a beer drinker? It's rare for someone to ask for a pop."

"Not anymore."

"Let me see what I can muster up for you." She turns and makes a big deal about swinging her hips. I roll my eyes. The girl will do anything for tips, it seems.

Then she bends over and I direct my attention to the Heineken sign, wonder if the Heineken execs are smiling down from heaven at this unnecessary advertisement. The fridge's door closes. I can feel the bartender's eyes on me.

As coolly as I can, I turn back to face her. I see she has a can of Coke in hand.

Sweet relief.

"Here you go, honey," she says.

I'm obviously older than this woman. She's probably in her late twenties so I have her by over a decade, I'm guessing. It's weird that she calls me honey. Always thought that was something reserved for couples and grandmas.

She pops the tab on the can. It makes a weak *fizzle* that both breaks my heart and brings back my hope in humanity. It's been so long since I've tasted Coca-Cola.

"Do you have a cup and some ice?" I ask. I know I'm really pushing it here. Ice? That's practically unheard of. Sure, they have a refrigerator, but why waste the electricity on freezing stuff, right?

"Sure, hon," she answers.

She gets a glass and scoops a few small cubes out of a bucket in an old sink. Health codes be damned. I don't care. This is great.

Then she's pouring the Coke into the glass and there's hardly any bubbles at all.

"It's cold already," she says.

"No, I'll wait until the ice does its job."

She smirks. She can see how hard that is for me. Waiting. I'm practically drooling. "All right," she says, "if there's anything else I can get you, just let me know."

"Will do," I say.

But the bartender doesn't go away. She hovers, like she's waiting for something. It takes me a moment to realize what that something is.

"Right," I say, never taking my eyes off of the glass. The man three stools down chuckles. "What's the damage?" It's a tough question. There's no such thing as paper money anymore. That stuff isn't worth anything. I knew a guy in Haven who once lived in a trailer park converted to a zombie defense outpost. He said him and his squadron ran out of toilet paper. The nearest store was cleaned out. But there was a bank. These guys broke into a vault and took cases of twenties, fifties, and hundreds back to their camp just so they wouldn't have to wipe their asses on old leaves. Imagine that. People literally wiping their asses with Ben Franklin's face.

The bartender is almost surely going to answer my question with—

"Well, what do you have? And you better not say nothing. There's hell to pay for people that steal drinks," she says. She speaks with a bit of good humor in her voice, but her eyes tell me she's not kidding.

I put my hands up defensively. "No worries," I say. I dig into my pocket again and pull out a small bottle of Excedrin. It's green and the label is a bit faded. The expiration date has long since passed. Doesn't matter much. They're not making it anymore. This stuff is vintage, and it still works. "Good for pain and aches, especially those of the head," I say. "Chew 'em for faster relief."

She picks it up and holds it to the light, then she shakes it. The pills rattle and cause a few curious heads to turn in our direction. "Still works?" she asks.

I nod. "Still works. Like a charm, I might add."

"Something like this is good for more than a Coke."

"I'll see how I'm feeling after this. Been a long time since I've enjoyed one of these. The sugar might not sit well with me," I say.

She laughs like I'm the funniest guy in the world, then she turns around, slipping the pill bottle into her front jeans pocket. She busies herself with cleaning, but this place needs more than a wipe down by a graying rag.

I sit on the stool and stare at my drink, thinking of my dead wife and son, thinking of Norm and Abby. That's what you do in a bar, right? You drown your sorrows, even if it's with Coca-Cola.

The day gets brighter and the few drunk guys inside leave.

"Excuse me, miss," I say.

She turns around, smiling. "Want a refill, sugar?" That last word just sounds wrong coming out of her mouth.

"No, thanks. I was just wondering where I could get some sleep."

"Travelers' Bay right on down the road." She

points to the wall on my left as if she can see through it, no doubt talking about the place I saw those men stumbling to earlier.

"How much for a room?"

She seems to contemplate this for a long moment, tonguing the inside of her cheek. She answers with what I think is her real voice, the one she uses when she's not trying to butter people up or get them drunk enough to let their most prized possessions slip into that front jeans pocket.

"For you," she says, "I can get you two nights free of charge." She pats the pill-shape in her pocket.

I nod. The Excedrin isn't a dud like the batteries I gave the guard, but it's not like old headache medicine is *that* hard to come by. Surely this woman knows this. Even if she's a little annoying, her deep blue eyes scream intelligence. So, instead, I take it that she likes me.

"Thank you," I say.

"No problem. Just go on in and tell the fellow there that Lilly says you're paid for." She sticks out her hand. I shake it.

"Jack," I say, "Jack Jupiter."

"Nice to meet you, Jack. I'm Lilliana, but you can call me Lilly like everyone else in Freeland does."

I smile. This one doesn't feel as bad or awkward.

I get up. The fat guy to my right is still nursing his beer, but his eyes are closed to slits. Judging by his slow, heavy breathing, he might be sleeping.

"I'll see you around," I say.

"You better."

I turn and head out the batwing doors, down the ramp, and back to the road. The town inside the walls is waking up. People walk along the street, most of them workers. Older men and women with harsh faces and worn clothes about them, some parents and their offspring—or most likely their adopted offspring. Nobody drives a car. The place isn't big enough for that, and I doubt they even have a working engine here or a means to get gas.

A couple people smile and nod at me, tipping their invisible hats. I have since lowered the hood of my cloak. I take it seeing an unfamiliar face, one as shanty as mine, with a hood on would not bode well with the locals. Might draw too much unwanted attention.

I get to the Travelers' Bay not too long after I pass a young lady clutching books to her side. Going to school, I think, and that's good. At least this place is trying to do some good.

Even if it doesn't matter much in the long run.

We all die in the end. We all get our throats slit and our heads shot.

Inside the motel or hotel or whatever it is, a cloud of smoke rushes out to meet me as I open the door. More smoke than The Jet had. I cough a couple times and wait for it to stop stinging my eyes before I go to the front desk. Behind it, sits an older man with a beard much grayer than mine. He is the cause of all this smoke. He has three cigarettes in his mouth. They look homemade, crooked, fat with tobacco in some places, skinny in other places.

"What can I do you for?" he asks, barely understandable with the cigarettes in his mouth.

"I need a room."

"That'll be eighteen shidings," he says, holding out his hand.

Shidings? I think to myself. That's a new one.

"Lilly down at The Jet says I'm paid up."

The old man squints at me, takes his feet off of the front counter. His boots hit the tiled floor heavily. Now he's leaning forward, squinting so hard he reminds me of the fat guy in the bar. "Paid up? Who does Lilly think she is? Paid up!" He barks laughter, which quickly morphs into a hacking fit of coughing. One of the cigarettes falls from his mouth, careens onto the floor, lost to my eyes behind the counter.

"Yeah," I say. "Lilly says I'm paid up. She says you can take it up with her if you don't believe me."

Squinting again. He doesn't care that he's lost a cigarette, there's two more still smoldering in each corner of his mouth. He waves a hand now, fanning away a fresh screen of smoke. "No, no, young man, I believe ya. Lilly wouldn't be dumb enough to lie to me, and neither would an outworlder like yourself." He grins, showing black and yellow teeth.

Outworlder. Another term I've heard before to describe me. I'm a vagrant, a drifter, the type of guy who bounces from place to place seemingly without a destination. That's okay. Let them think that. Let them all think that. But I do have a destination.

Revenge. Vengeance.

The man opens a drawer. It squeaks terribly, making me want to shove my fingers into my ears. Keys jingle as he pulls out a small ring. Attached to it is an orange tag that reads 213 and a long, black skeleton key.

"Here ya go, son," he says, handing it to me.

I take it, my mind already lost in the thoughts of a mattress, a pillow, and a blanket. A roof over my head. The only thing better than this would be the one-eyed man's head on a stake.

"If there's any trouble, if you or Lilly is lying,

then expect me to send Calvin up to your room." He snickers, like he's in on some great joke. "Lock your door if you want, that big buffoon will knock it off its hinges as easily as if it was made outta newspaper."

"Thanks," I say, picturing a guy big enough to knock a door clean off its hinges. The image that comes to mind is of the big fellow who was sitting three stools down from me in the bar. Something about him just oozes *henchman*.

I go up the steps. They creak beneath my feet and a fresh smell of dust and wood rushes up to meet me. It's a good smell, one that I've missed. It beats the outdoors and the lingering odors of zombie guts and sickness so prominent in the wilderness. On the second floor landing, I turn right and read the numbers. Someone screams in 209. The floor groans in 211. 212 is silent and so is 213. The key goes in the lock, the door opens.

The room is nothing to write home about—a single window, a single bed, and a nightstand with a Bible on top of it—but it looks like heaven to me. There's a toilet and a small shower with a pre-filled bucket hanging from the ceiling. I close the door and lock it. I take a shower. The water is lukewarm at best, but it does well to take the dirt away from my skin, the oil from my hair.

I draw the curtains to block out the sunlight. Strip off my towel and lie naked on the bed. Then I lay my pistol next to the pillow—another lesson I've learned traversing the wasteland. Never sleep without your weapon nearby. That's just how the world is now.

5

I awake to the sound of clamoring outside of my second story window.

There is a chill in the air, but my body is slick with sweat and the old sheets—that have probably never been washed in their existence—stick to my skin. The sun has gone down. The sky is dark, but the streets are not. Torches light them. Some of them are lit with fire while others are lit by electricity. It is a godsend to see electricity again.

It takes me a moment to gather my thoughts. The noises outside don't help. There are screams and shouts. I can't tell if they are out of pain or joy. My guess is the former, but I've been wrong before and am hopefully wrong right now. Still, I grip my pistol with a sweaty hand because I've learned it's better to be safe than sorry.

I sit up now and yawn, thinking back to my dreams. They aren't significant enough for me to remember, but I'm guessing they were nightmares. Almost always are.

Outside, someone is saying, "Make way! Make way!"

Speaking of nightmares, before Darlene and Junior were murdered, I suffered from the most horrible dreams imaginable, the type of nightmares one could never forget—believe me, I've tried very hard. All consisted of death. Once I dreamed about waking up next to Darlene. The sheets were soaked with warm liquid, but I'd never felt colder in my entire life. I patted the mattress, moved the covers, found Darlene. I remember in the dream, I shook her and said her name. She didn't answer. I was just about to turn on the light when I heard a tapping on our bedroom window. We didn't bother to put curtains up because we were on the second level. Because of this I saw the monster outside of the glass as plain as day. It was as if a spotlight had been shining on it's face. I can't say for sure, it might be the fact that many things have happened to me since those dreams, but I still think to this day that the one-eyed man had found a way to inhabit my subconscious mind. He held a bloody knife in one hand and Darlene's head in the other. She stared out at me with lifeless eyes. He tapped the knife's blade against the glass and said, *Jaaaaackkk, Jaaaacccck... JACK!* And the lights flipped on and I saw Darlene's headless body next to me. I saw that the warm liquid soaking through the sheets and my clothes was blood. Her blood.

I woke up screaming. Darlene was right next to me, unharmed. I don't know how many more nights we would've had together before the unspeakable happened to her and Junior and Haven, but it wasn't many.

Then something crazy *did* happen. At one of our council meetings Carmen, Darlene's sister, brought up the nightmares she'd been having. They had all dealt with death. Then Abby spoke up and Darlene did, too. Norm wouldn't admit to having the same nightmares as us, but his husband Tim did. Not only did they deal with death, but they had something else in common, too. There was a man in all of them. This man was older, his face was wrinkled and worn like he'd seen more bloodshed than all of us combined. In my dreams, he was missing his eye; in Darlene's he was missing a nose; in Abby's a hand like her; in Norm's he was whole (we knew this to be an obvious lie). And so on and so on. Norm still wasn't convinced of our shared dreams, he had said it was some fantastical bullshit and I would've been inclined to agree with him had zombies not infested our world. If that was possible, anything is.

Then, not too long after Haven had fallen, and I'd seen that face from my dreams brought to reality. The one-eyed man, the leader of the radical group calling themselves the District, the one who took my family from me.

He had help. I've found some of those bastards.

Like I've said before, I have not let any of them live.

I'm up now, getting my pants back on, my shirt, my cloak. The rambling outside has picked up, but I'm not quick to check it out. Frankly, I don't care much. In my experience any noise after sundown is never a good thing.

It can't be a flood of zombies from a breach in the gates, either. If it was, there'd be a lot more screaming.

Once I'm dressed, I go downstairs, taking the creaky steps one at a time. There's a clamor coming from the first level of the motel, men and women talking in hushed tones. It's dark down here, too.

Shadows dance across the floor from a single candlelight burning at the front desk. The old man still sits behind it, but his feet aren't up. He doesn't look the least bit relaxed, though he's still smoking. Just one cigarette tonight.

I see the windows are shuttered and the door is barred closed.

"Might as well go back up to your room, sir, and get some shut-eye," the old man says to me.

"What's going on?" I ask. My fingers tingle as my post-apocalyptic senses tell me I should fill my hand with a weapon.

"Don't want to know, outlander," the old man says.

"I do. That's why I asked."

Someone in the lobby area chuckles. "He got you there, Franky."

"Aw, stuff it, Rich, or I'll kick you out and make you see them District boys face to face," the old man says.

My heart shudders to a stop. I arch an eyebrow, trying not to let the surprise show on my face. So I ask as nonchalantly as possible, "District?"

"What are you, a dummy?" Franky asks, looking at me cross-eyed.

"Be nice," a woman says to the left of the bottom

of the stairs. I look over, thinking it might be the bartender Lilliana. It's not. It's a woman in her fifties or sixties with silver hair. Her skin is porcelain smooth, no lines or wrinkles whatsoever. I'm reminded of Eve, Darlene's mother, who was the leader of Haven and the founder of the council we were on before she died of what the compound's doctors diagnosed as cancer. It was a nasty affair. Without proper treatment, Eve withered away to basically nothing. It had hurt Darlene and her sister Carmen very badly. Hell, it hurt every last one of Haven's citizens.

"Don't tell me what to do, woman!" Frank yells.

"Quiet!" Rich hisses.

There's a handful of others in the room, but they look too scared to speak. Their faces are pale, their heads are stooped.

"I'm going to get a drink," I say, and walk through the lobby.

Rich steps in front of me. He's a man about my age, somewhere in his forties. He's burly, clean-shaven, short-cropped hair covered by a Sherlock Holmes hat. There's nothing about him that's intimidating, I think, until I look into his eyes. There is a primal fear in those eyes, and the reason he's so frightened, the reason the door is barred and the shades are drawn, is because he, along with everyone else in this lobby, is afraid of the District.

I don't blame them.

But I'm not scared. Not many things scare me anymore. Before I lost Darlene and Junior, the only thing that did scare me was losing my family. Now I'm a man with nothing left to lose.

"Please, sir, don't go out there. For all our sakes," Rich says.

"If he wants to be a dumbass, let him be a dumbass," Frank says. I do my best to ignore it. No need to pick a fight with a crotchety old man. "If you think about it, he'll be a distraction. Them District boys will set their sights on him and forget about us." He closes his eyes then mumbles something that reminds me of a silent prayer. This is all but confirmed when he does the sign of the cross right in front of me.

"Please," Rich says again, ignoring Franky. "Please, sir, I don't know you, but I know there's not a lot of us left. No reason to get yourself killed."

"You see his sword, Rich?" the woman asks. "He isn't going to die. Not Conan the Barbarian here." She chuckles and a score of the other formerly silent people echo her laughter.

I'm not amused. Not many things amuse me these days.

"I appreciate the concern," I say to Rich, "but I'm parched. I could really use a drink."

"We have—"

I don't let Rich finish, no time to listen to bullshit. If the District is here, I have to make them pay. So I push past him, cutting him off, and open the door to the fire-lit streets beyond.

But when I look up, the man I see out there makes me want to go back inside.

6

I don't go back in the motel for obvious reasons, the biggest of them being that I've already made a big fuss about being brave and I have to stick to that.

Still, it's hard to be brave sometimes.

The man I see has his back turned toward me then he disappears into The Jet.

The man's name is Brandon. He was there when Haven fell. He was there when Darlene's throat was slit and my boy was shot in the back of the head. He was there laughing and cheering the one-eyed man on. He helped hold Darlene down. She had put up such a fight.

I start to shake. Tears blur my vision. Not because I'm sad, but because I'm angry. More angry than I realize.

I take a deep breath. Get it together, Jack. Compose yourself.

I know if I go in there guns-a-blazing, it will not end well for any of us. Innocent bystanders will probably be killed. I'll have to play this right.

Going up the street, I pass buildings with blinds drawn and doors locked just like the Travelers' Bay, except I see faces poking out through the curtains and shutters. Pale faces and wide eyes.

My heels click on the old asphalt.

I am a lone gunslinger (with a sword) coming down a dusty street to pick a fight with the black hat.

Just before I get to the downed plane, I hear something that causes me to draw my pistol and raise it up. It's a sound predisposed to make my trigger finger convulse. It's the groans and moans of zombies. A pack, by the sound of it.

I take cover at the corner of the abandoned post office. Gaze around.

My jaw drops.

The zombies are chained up, attached to a car. It's not a normal car, though. It's sawed in half. The front end of a convertible with an extra wheel added to the back part near the seats so it looks like a tricycle. The metal is jagged and dangerously sharp. The windshield is cracked and slick with dark blood.

The hood ornament is gone, but judging by what's left of the body, it's a Chrysler. Another blast from the past.

I now see why the zombies are there. I have to squint. They are missing their bottom jaws and the teeth in the upper part has been removed. Each hand is nothing but a bloody hunk of flesh, no fingers so they can't scratch. Their eyes burn as fervently as ever, though, and as soon as they see me or smell me, they lunge forward, causing the car to creak. It goes nowhere. Thank God for the parking brake…I think.

Still, I'm unnerved. Only people—hell, I don't know if I should even call them that—who would be crazy enough to hook a pack of rotters up to a sawed-off convertible are people from the District.

I holster my gun, knowing the zombies aren't a threat and probably never will be unless someone has an irrational fear of being gummed to death, of which I do not.

I go up the ramp to The Jet and push through the batwing doors. No piano plays, but the same man from earlier sits at the bench, his posture stooped, his eyes averted to the floor. Lilliana is behind the bar with another woman, this one older than her. They rush back and forth with drinks in their hands.

I catch eyes with Lilly as she comes out from behind the bar with three glasses of flat beer, filled to the brim. Her eyes practically plead for me to get out of here.

I'm not leaving. I'm thirsty.

Thirsty for blood.

Lilly brings those beers to the corner booth where the District have set up shop in the corner of the large room . Brandon has his back turned to me still, but I know it's him. I could recognize that misshaped head a mile away. He's a little younger. Probably in his early thirties. He has that certain kind of cockiness commonly seen in the big man on campus back in high school and college. As Lilliana sets the glasses down, he reaches out and slaps her ass with a big, dirty hand. Lilly stiffens at the gesture. I can only see the side of her face, but the way her eyes bore into him and her lips raise in a snarl tells me she is not particularly fond of Brandon's greeting.

One of the other District officers sees me eyeing the table and leans over and whispers to a different officer, who turns to look at me just before I make a show of hailing down the other bartender.

I have to play this right. I'm outnumbered here.

But how do I play it?

"I'd like a Coca-Cola, please," I say.

The woman gives me a tired look. "I'm sorry," she says, "Coca-Cola and other sweet beverages aren't for public consumption."

Just as I'm about to argue and say *Well, Lilly gave me one less than twenty-four hours ago,* I feel a hand on my shoulder.

"Jack. Nice to see you again. What'll it be? The usual?" Lilly asks.

I blink stupidly up at her. The usual? I'm not a regular. I'm not—

"Whiskey, right?" Lilly says. She gives me a slight wink. The other bartender has lost interest in the conversation. I decide to just go with the flow. Can't afford to stick out with the District here.

I stammer, "Y-Yeah, the usual."

"Jack Daniels coming right up," Lilly says.

The other bartender rolls her eyes and moves out of Lilly's way as a fresh highball glass is put in front of me and filled with smooth whiskey. I pick it up and put my mouth to the rim. It burns on its way down, feels like a fire in my belly. "Ah," I say. "Thanks, Lilly."

"No problem," she answers. Then she's gone as quick as she came, back tending to the other customers, filling up glasses and smiling as well as she can with the added pressure of having stone-cold killers as her newest patrons.

"Hey there, piano man!" Brandon yells. His other goons laugh. "Play us a song!"

The man on the piano bench jumps at the sound of Brandon's voice, then he stutters and stumbles over his words. "S-Sure, friends! What'll it b-be?"

"Surprise me," Brandon says.

More laughter from his goons. A sour feeling arises in the pit of my stomach. My grip on my glass tightens enough that I think I might accidentally shatter it into a million pieces. Talk about lying low, huh? I take another deep breath to compose myself, trying not to think about my dead wife and son, or Norm and Abby and all those other Havenites who had their lives taken from them.

The piano starts up. It's a song I don't immediately recognize. My head is too fuzzy for me to pinpoint it. That's okay. I'm not here to listen to music. I'm here to get one step closer to my ultimate goal of revenge.

Judging by Brandon's already slurring words, he and his friends have had more than a few drinks before coming to The Jet. A few more and I'll make my move.

7

Then something happens, something that changes my plans.

Brandon is up, screaming at the piano player. "Play Billy Joel!"

And the piano player says "I don't know any Billy Joel."

Brandon hits him, knocks him off his bench. "How the fuck don't you know any Billy Joel? You call yourself a piano man?" Then he's laughing and wailing on him.

The other District guards stand up and draw their weapons, aiming them at anyone who makes a move to stop Brandon.

"Lucky it's not you on the ground," one of them

says as a man lunges forward. "Sit back down or you get a bullet in the brain." He cocks the hammer.

I may not have hope in humanity anymore, but that doesn't mean I have to sit around and put up with this bullshit.

So I move fast because I have to. I kick the stool out in front of me, and it careens in the direction of the goons. Wood splinters as it connects with the goon's knee, taking his legs out from under him, and his gun hits the floor. It clanks and cartwheels off somewhere to my left. Most importantly, out of the goon's reach. Then, because I really don't want to waste my own ammunition on the likes of a grunt, I pull my sword free from its scabbard. It has seen a lot of zombie flesh in its line of duty, not much human. Today it meets the other goon's neck. I do this in one quick motion, pulling the hidden blade out from beneath my cloak. The edge swipes across the area just below the man's chin. I don't think I have enough power behind it to kill him, but the spray of blood and the wheezing that follows tells me I'm wrong. This goon is big and as he falls, he makes quite the racket, though the screams from the bar's crowd are much louder. Goon lands on other goon, pins him to the ground.

Good. This buys me more time.

Unfortunately, I don't have much of it to admire the beautiful mess I've made. And though, I'm not a fan of killing humans, I understand these men deserve it for their affiliation with the District alone. Add the mountains of wrongdoings these men have done, the destruction they've left in their wake, the innocent blood they've spilled, and I'm doing the world a big favor.

My heart plummets and my stomach flips as I whirl around.

Here is Brandon. His mouth hangs wide open. He has stopped kicking the piano player. The man on the ground is unconscious, blood streaming from his chin in strings, rivulets leaking from his nose. Brandon fumbles at the gun on his belt. Probably the booze. Expired though it may be, it's potent enough. Thank God.

I throw my sword at him. For as big as it is, it's surprisingly light. I aim for his gun hand, but my aim is off the slightest bit. Instead of the bicep, I hit him in the shoulder. The sword goes clean through, pins him to the wood of the piano. Right now, I'm grateful it's there because there's no way the blade is sharp enough to penetrate the metal walls of what used to be a military plane.

Brandon yells in pain and anger. His gun clatters

to the ground. One of the nearby drinkers is smart enough to kick it out of the way. I give him a thankful nod.

Now I pull my own pistol free. Flashes of that horrible night come to me in a rush. Brandon is there holding Darlene down on her knees as the blood pours out from between her laced fingers. She holds the red smile beneath her chin. She gasps for air that won't stay in her throat. How bright everything is, even in the darkness. Then Junior thrown to the ground. The man with one eye stomping his boot down on his spine. My son, my thirteen year old son. The boy. A part of me. Then the one-eyed man not even looking down at Junior as he pulls the trigger. Me screaming until my lungs burn and my vocal cords snap. The flash of the gunshot. So bright. The spray of blood. Brighter. My son's screaming and crying cut off.

Forever.

The now is a blur, but I'm back, and I'm shaking the gun in Brandon's face, crying and yelling at him about Darlene and Junior.

Brandon grimaces and says, "I don't know what the fuck you're talking about, you crazy motherfucker."

And I say, "Yes you do. You were there."

He opens his mouth to reply, but I don't want to hear him talk anymore. Nothing he can say will bring back my wife and son. So I bring the gun across my body and slap him in the face with the jagged metal. A red cut appears instantly beneath his left eye, then his head lolls and his eyes roll back. He is unconscious.

Movement behind me.

Words thrown in my direction.

"You son of a bitch. I'll fucking kill—" the other goon yells.

I don't care to hear what this man has to say, either. I pull the trigger. My aim is true. The bullet released from my pistol blasts a hole in his face, and he doesn't talk from this hole. He dies instantly, which is better than anyone from the District deserves.

Now there's a silence as the echo of my gunshot dies out. Every eye is on me.

I look to Lilliana and the other bartender. Lilly isn't scared anymore; she has seen this kind of death and destruction before, but the other bartender is petrified. I have never been good with people in the first place. In Haven, Darlene and Abby gladly took the diplomatic duties from me. Despite this obvious flaw, I offer up my voice.

"I'll help clean this up," I say.

No one else says anything. I wonder if they're as afraid of me and I'm afraid of myself.

Then I look to Lilliana and say, "Do you have any rope?"

Finally someone else speaks up. It's the man who has kicked Brandon's gun out of his reach—not that that matters much now.

"What do you mean rope? Just finish the job," he says.

"No. I got bigger plans for this one," I say, and I do.

Lilly disappears behind the counter. I think for a second that she is going to pull a shotgun out from beneath the bar and blow a hole through my sternum.

She doesn't.

Instead, she pulls a thick length of rope out and tosses it in my direction.

"Thanks," I tell her.

I pull my sword free and wipe Brandon's blood off on his shirt. He stands for a moment then falls hard on the floor, so hard that a few discordant notes play from the piano. I flip him over with my boot. He groans. He'll be conscious quick enough. Lucky for me my brother Norman has taught me how to tie knots that are all but impossible to get out of.

I tie Brandon up in one of these knots. He's not going anywhere. I take a step back to admire my work. Norm would be proud. I miss the son of a bitch.

The end of the rope in hand, my gun on my right hip and the sword sheathed on my back, I drag Brandon out of The Jet. He leaves a trail of blood in his wake, and I turn around and tell Lilly and the other woman that I'll be back to help clean.

As I go down the ramp, two guards pull up to me on horses, their weapons drawn.

I don't flinch, don't stop, don't put my hands up. I just keep on dragging Brandon behind me. "Don't worry," I say to these guards. "I've got it handled."

"You're in our jurisdiction," one guard says and he has the gruff voice I recognize from the watch tower. I wonder if he has discovered the batteries I gave him were duds. Probably not. If that were the case, I think he would've shot me already. "Drop the rope. You're under arrest."

The other guard's eyes shift from me to his partner. The horses are spooked. They can smell the zombies waiting around the corner of the downed jet and the blood leaking out from the batwing doors.

"I'm not under arrest," I say. "I did your job for you. If anything, you should be giving me a deputy star and shaking my hand."

The nervous guard is older than me. There's wisdom behind the nervousness in his eyes.

"He's right, Curly," this guard says. "He ain't under arrest. He's obviously got business he's got to handle—"

"I don't care if he is Jesus Christ reincarnated, Bill. He killed people. *District* people," the guard named Curly says.

"I did you a favor. Now quit pointing your gun at me and get out of my way," I say. I really don't have time for these post-apocalyptic rent-a-cops.

Bill, the wiser of the two guards, dismounts from his horse. "Here," he says, "he's all yours. You get out of here and don't come back, we'll let you walk."

"Bill," Curly snaps, but Bill holds up a hand to stop the younger guard's protests.

"Go on," Bill says to me.

I nod, bend down and lift Brandon up onto my shoulder. He's still unconscious and though he's quite scrawny, dead weight weighs a lot. I sling him over the horse's backside while I tie the extra rope around the saddle. It has been a long time since I've ridden a horse.

"Bilbo," Bill says. "That's the horse's name. He's a sweet thing. He'll treat you right. I wish you the best of luck on your journey. *Both* of you." Bill approaches the horse and rubs the space between his eyes. The horse whinnies.

"No, I can't take your horse," I say.

"Anyone brave enough to stand up to the District deserves more than this," Bill says.

I can see he's not giving up.

"Thank you," I say.

Slowly, I mount Bilbo. He doesn't buck or quiver at my touch. In fact, he's perfectly fine with me on top him.

Curly is frowning, scratching his head, glaring at me. "You better not come back. We mean it."

I say nothing and tip an invisible hat in Bill's direction. Now on the horse's back, I snap the reins lightly and guide him back the way I came in. Out of the corner of my eye, I see Lilliana and the rest of the bar patrons clustered near the ramp and the batwing doors. I can't tell if there's fear or admiration in their gazes.

As I approach the gates, leaving two dead District goons and a trail of blood in my wake, I hear

Bill shout, "Let him through! Let him through!" He's now on Curly's horse with him. They're not far behind.

The gate creaks open as whoever is up there cranks the handle that turns the tires and raises the fence.

I spur Bilbo onward. He takes off at the sight of the open road. Then the wind snaps through both my too-long hair and my too-long beard.

8

It does not take long before a stray zombie appears on the path. I steer Bilbo out of its way. I think it's a woman. Can't tell for sure. The horse runs much too fast, but that's good. Behind me, Brandon is starting to come back into consciousness, moaning in pain, mumbling something about the burning in his shoulder. I don't answer him.

Him and I will talk soon enough.

I've seen the one zombie so I think it's safe to assume there is more around these parts. There always is. I pull up on the reins to slow Bilbo down. He doesn't seem happy that I've done it. The horse wants to run like the wind and I don't blame him for wanting that. We go off the cracked asphalt, his steady *clop-clopping* is now muffled by grass and dirt.

I guide him slowly through a path between the dark trees, which stand tall and vigilant like guards of the forest.

The utter blackness here is nice. It's home.

We ride for nearly fifteen minutes before I find what I'm looking for.

A clearing in the forest on a slight rise. There's one dead oak in the middle of this clearing, as if God has put it there just for me, a notion I know is both ridiculous and borderline crazy.

I guide Bilbo up the hill to the dead tree. I whisper, "Good boy," to him. I'm not sure how one talks to a horse, so I go off of instinct. I once had a dog in Haven. His name was Cupcake. We had many good years before old age eventually took him. He died in my arms, peacefully. Though not a horse, Cupcake responded very well to praise. Seems like Bilbo does the same. He likes me and I don't like that. Can't get attached. There's no point in getting attached in this world.

At the top of the hill, I dismount. I tell the horse to stay, he doesn't listen. I have to tie him up to the other side of the tree without much slack. He'll get a front row seat to this show.

Then I'm dragging Brandon to the base of the tree, sitting him up against the trunk. He's groggy, but his eyes are fluttering open. I start working on his binds, untying everything but his hands and feet. With the extra rope I have, I'm able to wrap it around the tree's trunk and knot it. Just as I'm doing this, Brandon says, "Where the fuck am I?"

I round the trunk and reply, "I wouldn't be too loud if I were you. These woods are crawling with the dead."

"Who the fuck are you?" he spits.

"You know who I am."

"No, I really don't," Brandon says.

I kneel and draw my blade.

"Oh, I see, you're some wacko with a sword. Pinch me, I must be dreaming."

A grin spreads on my face. That's cute. Brandon hasn't lost any of his asshole-ish charm.

I flip the sword around and press on Brandon's wound with the hilt. He screams loud enough to stir the birds out of their sleep. They take to the sky, flapping their wings furiously, as they caw into the night.

I ease up.

"You piece of shit," he seethes. "As soon as I get out of here, I'm going to slit your throat like the Overlord slit your wife's."

Rage blinds me. Those words he spoke bring a

taste of hot bile up my throat. In this blind moment of fury, I am not sure what I do to him. Distantly, I hear his screams, I hear thuds, skin connecting with skin, the horse whinnying.

As I come back down to earth, I am panting. My fists are slick with blood. They sting and burn, like cracked and bleeding lips.

Brandon has a smile on his face. Red outlines each tooth like extended gums. He laughs. It's a wet laugh, thick with blood, pain.

"Yeah, I recognize ya. Took me a minute to realize it was you with that raccoon's ass of a beard on your face." Brandon laughs again. I resist the urge to kill him right here on the spot. Somewhere in the forest, I am dimly aware of a twig snapping underfoot. He leans over, still tied, still at my disposal, and spits a wad of blood onto the long blades of grass. It shimmers in the moonlight. Somehow, though, it feels as if I've lost control of this situation, just as I had lost control of the situation at Haven.

No. No, I can't let him get in my head.

"Shut up," I tell him. "The dead will hear you."

"Bring 'em on," Brandon says. A wild look invades his eyes, almost zombie-like in nature. "Hear me? Bring those cocksuckers on!" he shouts. His voice carries, echoes in the hills.

Jesus, this guy is crazier than I remember.

There's a momentary lull in our conversation. I'm staring at him, unsure of what to do. I should just kill him. Just end it so I don't have to see that terrible face any longer.

But deep down inside I know I'll never forget his face for as long as I live. I won't forget any of the faces that had a hand in killing my wife and son, in kicking my life right out from beneath me.

"What you want with me? Jupiter, is it?"

I nod.

"What you want with me, Jupiter?"

"Information," I say.

Brandon grins again. "Only information I have that you would wanna know is what me and the boys did to your wife's corpse when you was passed out."

My blood freezes. I resist the urge to double over and be sick. Nausea has invaded me, nausea and hate. More hate than I knew I was capable of.

"Yeah, that was quite a fun time. How we passed her back and forth. The dead chicks will let you do anything to them. And I mean *anything*—"

I hit him, can't listen to that any longer. Then I breathe slowly, trying to keep cool.

"Any position. Any hole. You name it—"

I hit him again. It's hard not to kill him right now. It's possibly the hardest thing I've ever done. I have to change the subject, have to get down to business.

"I want information on the one-eyed man," I demand.

"Good luck finding it."

I smile now. I'm in control here. I have to remember that. "How much more pain do you think you can take?" I ask. How calmly these words come out surprises me. "I've only just pressed your wound with the hilt of this sword here. What do you think will happen when I stick the blade in and *twist*?"

Brandon's face goes stone-smooth.

"Let's find out, shall we?" I turn the sword on him and aim for the bleeding gash in his shoulder. He winces, tries to pull back away from me, but is blocked by the tree. I hover right above the wound. The edge winks in the moonlight. Behind, a groan creeps up the hill.

"Ah, our first guest has arrived," I say, turning around. "It's a dinner party." I give Brandon a wink. "You're the main course."

A zombie in tattered clothes shambles toward us.

Her eyes are blazing with hunger. As she gets closer, I see her jaw hanging by strands of sinew, muscle, and bone. It swings back and forth like a pendulum. She may not be too successful in chewing on Brandon, but her upper teeth are as sharp as ever.

More flood out from the surrounding trees. Luckily, we have the high ground. If we didn't I would have already gotten the hell out of here.

I look to Brandon. His stony expression has vanished. Now his eyes are wide, full of tears. Seeing this man quivering like a frightened puppy almost makes me feel bad for him.

Almost.

It's the sight of all the zombies that make him look this way. There's a lot.

I wonder if these zombies are locals, people infected by the virus or bitten by their loved ones, doomed to roam these woods until someone comes along and puts a bullet or a blade between their eyes.

"Let me out of here, man," Brandon suddenly says in a weak voice. It surprises me.

Bilbo, on the other side of the tree, whinnies and wickers. Time is short. I'll have to act fast.

"Not until you tell me what I want to know," I say.

The first zombie is only a few feet away from me. Her sights are set on Brandon—thankfully. The zombies seem to evolve, at least the slightest bit. They know when getting their sustenance will be a challenge. To put it simply: don't attack the guy holding a large sword.

I step out of the way and let the zombie get close enough to Brandon for her smell to engulf both of us. It's a terrible smell. I'm sure I've described it before. It's the smell of spoiled meat, of sickness.

Just as she lunges at Brandon, I stick my foot out and trip her.

She lands with a wet thud in the grass. One arm is outstretched. Dead, sickly-gray fingers wrap around Brandon's boot. He kicks out, but she's not letting go. She's practically superglued on. It seems she has some upper body strength left, too, because she pulls herself closer to him despite all of his kicking.

As this is happening, more are making their way up the hill. They are only coming up the same way this first zombified woman has come up. Not the smartest creatures, these zombies. I scan around the rest of the hill to make sure. So far, we're good. None are coming for neither I or Bilbo.

After what Brandon said about Darlene and

Haven, I suppose it's all right for me to have a little fun with this. After what he *did*.

Yes, get answers. I know.

That's the next step.

Now the other hand finds his crotch and Brandon squeals like a pig.

"Please!" he shouts. "Please! I'll tell you anything you want."

"Where is the one-eyed man?" I say.

From the crotch, this dead hand finds a coil of rope wrapped around Brandon's chest. A firm grasp and a desperate pull, and this zombie is breathing death right into his face.

"Ohio!" he shouts.

I suddenly think I'm going to be sick again.

Ohio? I thought I was done with that dreadful place.

"Where at in Ohio?"

Brandon tries to flatten himself up against the oak. No luck. "P-P-Please! Get it off me!"

I grab the zombie by her greasy, dirt-caked hair and yank backward. She lands on the tip of my blade. Brains leak from this fresh hole and the death rattling in the back of her throat ends along with her second life.

"There's your freebie," I say. "The next one that

gets that close, well, I'm going to let it take a hearty bite."

I know. I'm sick. I'm sadistic. Guilt turns my skin icy and I hate myself, but then I look at Brandon's face and I see what sick and sadistic truly is.

"So, Brandon, tell me more." I make a show of looking relaxed. I'm anything but relaxed.

"I told you all I know!" he says. "He's in Ohio. There's a place he found through one of his *visions!* It's called Leering."

Before he's finished his sentence, my stomach drops lower than ever. I didn't think it was possible. Leering Research Facility, now there's truly a blast from the past, and it's right on the edge of my old hometown.

It's times like these that I think life truly *is* one big circle. We always end up back where we started.

We shall see, but the feeling in the pit of my stomach tells me that it's affirmative.

Brandon stares at me, waiting for me to set him free. I believe him because he's scared to death. I can see it in his eyes, in his pale face. It's funny, really, how men turn to mice when they're stripped of their weapons and tied to a tree as zombie bait.

I've got all I need to know. It's not like the one-eyed man is hiding. I know exactly where Leering is

—or *was*. Last I heard, it had burned down. I wonder in the six months I'd been on the road since I'd last been in Woodhaven if some shady organization like Central had tried to salvage all of its secrets. It wouldn't surprise me.

Groans behind again.

I spin around and lop off the head of a naked zombie much too close to Bilbo and I. The body crumbles to a pile of dust as soon as my blade makes contact. Poor bastard, I'm thinking, how unfortunate to turn without your clothes on. I'd at least have the decency to put on a robe if I knew where my sickness was heading. Not everyone is as wise as me, I guess.

"Oh, thank God," Brandon breathes. He's beyond on-edge.

"There's another freebie. I want to know more," I say, wiping the blade off on Brandon's head. Goo and dried brains settled on his curly, dark hair like a hat.

I know, I know. I'm a monster. All that bullshit.

"Anything! Anything you want, Jupiter!" he shouts.

But I don't know what to ask him. So I say the first thing that comes to mind. "Why? Why did he do it?"

Brandon's brow furrows, causing the zombie

dandruff to cascade down his face. "Why did who do what?"

"You know who. You know what," I say.

Brandon closes his eyes, takes a shaky breath. "Jupiter, is that really the question you want to ask me right now?"

I nod.

I can already feel the zombies closing in behind me. Their guttural howls, their unnerving footsteps. Right now, I don't care. Right now, I am invincible.

"Why did he do it? Why did you follow him?"

Brandon stares past me at the zombies. I step back, but I don't slice and dice. Not yet. Have to keep the fear ingrained in him.

"Answer me," I demand.

The nearest zombie lunges at Brandon. I grab the creature's waistband. This man has died and come back wearing sweatpants, thank God. The elastic hasn't snapped or rotted. So it's like having the zombie on a bungee cord as he flails his scabby arms at Brandon and clamps his jaws open and closed with a click loud enough to be heard over the chorus of zombie voices.

Bilbo is prancing, trying to get away. Soon, my new friend, soon.

Brandon screams and turns his head. I give the

zombie a little more slack. He's inches away from Brandon's ear.

"This one is hungry!" I shout. "Answer the question and I'll throw him down the hill. Do a little zombie bowling."

"He did it because he just enjoys chaos! And we followed him because…"

I push the zombie forward. His face makes contact with Brandon's. Brandon screams bloody murder, shrill enough to make me want to cringe away. The zombie, lucky for Brandon, doesn't take a chunk out of his cheek. The sudden movement confuses the beast. All that Brandon has to show for this incident is a smeared red mark that isn't his blood.

"Followed him because why?" I shout, pulling the zombie back again.

"Because he's crazy enough to thrive in this fucked up world!" Brandon shouts. "Because he has a way with words!"

That sounds about right. People think there's safety in crazy. Look at Germany following Hitler. Sometimes they're so scared, they can't sense the crazy they're choosing to follow until it's too late.

It's good enough. The zombie meets my blade and stops struggling.

"It's all about survival," Brandon babbles. "They think he's the best bet at surviving."

I nod. There's one more question on my mind. I ask it. "Everyone in Haven. When I woke up, everyone was either dead or gone. What happened to the others?"

Brandon smiles. His eyes don't. In those eyes there is still fear. "What do you think happened to them?" I think they're still out there. Somewhere. They have to be.

I point the blade, slick with zombie blood, at his open wound. He knows as well as I do that if that blood gets into his own blood stream, he's only got a few hours before he turns, but he doesn't wince at this. It's quite dissatisfying.

"They went with him, with *us*. They drank the fucking Kool-Aid. Do you blame them?" Brandon says.

No way. That's impossible.

I think of Norm and Abby, part of the few bodies among the ruins I did not find. Some of the deceased were desiccated, but not beyond recognition. I scoured the remains. I scoured the whole park. It took me nearly two weeks to do this, to find and bury all of the dead. I was so sore afterward, I could hardly walk, but I couldn't just lie down. Back then, I was stupid enough to keep going. So I did. I killed any zombies that found their way through the blown-away gates. Beat any others who I'd stumbled upon feasting on the corpses. I was an angry man then. I was hotheaded.

Not any longer.

Now, I am a numb man.

Still, I cannot see Norm and Abby joining up with the one-eyed man and the District, those who had killed their loved ones and destroyed their homes.

I look at Brandon, hate in my eyes. "Why did he leave me alive?"

"Oh, finally! An easy one!" Brandon chuckles.

The nearest zombie lunges and I slice it in half with a grunt. A spray of blood soaks my pants, chills me. How it is so cold, I have no clue, especially when the days have been warm and the nights barely chilly.

"He wanted you to see what he'd done," Brandon says. "He wanted you to wake up and take it all in."

"Why me?"

Brandon smiles slyly. I have stared into the face of evil countless times before. I can recognize it from a mile away. In this day and age, there are more evil men and women than there are good, it seems. But

Brandon...he is beyond evil. He is way past a point of no return.

"You, because he dreamed about you," Brandon says. "You, because you threatened him."

"I didn't even know him."

"Didn't matter."

"Does he still dream about me?"

"I highly doubt it. You're not exactly important anymore. I mean, look at you. You look like death reincarnated. Like that *thing*." Brandon nods at a zombie close behind me. I turn around to be greeted with a gruesome sight. One arm. A chest that's caved in, an exposed blackened heart. The snarling face, lips peeled back, teeth bloody. I kill the thing before it has a chance to lunge.

"I haven't seen the Overlord for many a moon. It's not my destiny to see him any longer," Brandon says. His face goes slack, as if he's repeating a prayer he's memorized. There's a blank, dead look in his eyes. "No, I've seen the future and I'm not in it. Isn't that right, Jupiter?"

Goosebumps prickle my flesh. This isn't right. This whole experience is wrong. I don't know what's going on, what Brandon is doing to me.

"Thank you, Jupiter. Thank you for giving me what I want. Thank you, thank you, thank you! The

Overlord thanks you, too." He starts to shake, to writhe like a snake. I take a step back. Cold flesh touches my hand. I turn around.

More zombies.

I nearly fall just as one reaches out for me.

"Your friends are one of us, Jupiter!" Brandon is shouting. "You can be, too. I'm sure he'd welcome you with open arms...if you *let* him."

The words barely register in my brain because I'm reaching for my gun, almost dropping my sword, too, as I swing it as hard as I can in a semicircle. Blood splashes. Limbs dice.

The gun in my hand now. I aim up, blow the face off of the nearest zombie. All that's left standing in front of me is a mounting mess of gore. I'm quick on the trigger. True on the aim. Three more drop, double-dead.

"It's okay, Jupiter. Let him in. Let him in!" Brandon says. My heart has either beat so hard its exploded in my chest or I'm more numb than numb. Now that I have cleared some room, I turn around and rush toward Bilbo. Two zombies have spotted the horse and make their way toward him.

Two more shots. Horse is not on the menu tonight.

Brandon doesn't scream as a few zombies fall to

the ground before him. It's all happening in slow motion, eerie opera music playing in my head. The spray of the reddest blood I've ever seen exploding from his jugular. The twitching of his neck as flesh is torn and stretched beyond its capability, drowning out the opera music with a wet and audible *snap*. The whole time this goes on, Brandon's eyes never leave mine. There's knowledge in those eyes. Maybe it's the knowledge of death. Maybe it's the knowledge of the future. I can't say for sure. All I do know is that it creeps me out, scares me beyond belief.

Bilbo is tied to the tree and I literally don't have time to untie his reins. If I try, the zombies would fall on us quicker than they've fallen on Brandon. So I slice down with my sword and the reins snap at the touch of the blade's edge. As soon as I jump onto Bilbo's back, he lifts up on his hind legs, kicking his front ones out in defense. A few more zombies have snaked around the tree trunk, knowing they're too late to the dinner party that is Brandon. I can't even distinguish their features, they are too old and weathered. Ancient corpses. Unholy. Unnatural.

"Go! Go!" I shout at Bilbo, but he doesn't need me to tell him. He lands and, in a burst of speed, bowls over the zombies. Their death radiates off of them in waves. I feel it on my skin, as cold as the Grim Reaper's touch. Down the hill we go, me hanging on for dear life, leaving the zombies behind, leaving Brandon to his demise.

What unnerves me the most throughout our entire descent is that I never hear him scream.

Not even once.

9

Bilbo gallops until we are clear of the forest, back on the road again. I don't think I've taken a breath since we left that horde.

I pull on what's left of Bilbo's reins. "Whoa," I say. I need to catch my breath and so does the horse. We are on a bridge, water rushing beneath us in a steady roar. It sounds like some runaway monster.

I spur him on at a trot. This isn't the place we should be. Hearing is everything in the apocalypse. My ears are tuned to listen for the slightest out of place noise, but if I can't hear anything over the roar of the water, it'll make no difference. Anyone or *anything* could sneak up on us.

Just as we cross the bridge and hit solid road again, I do hear something. My gun comes out in a blur and aims down the dark woods where I think I heard the sound.

It's footsteps.

"Not again," I say. "Fucking zombies."

But it's not a zombie. It's a woman, and she comes out with her hands held high above her head. "Don't shoot," she pleads.

It takes a moment for me to register who the woman is, and once I do, I can't believe it.

"Lilly?" I say.

"Hi," she replies. "I didn't mean to spook you."

"You've been following me." It's not a question.

"I had to get out of there," she says. She approaches Bilbo and strokes the bridge of his nose. What you call that on a horse, I have no idea. Snout? Muzzle? I'll settle with muzzle.

"Not safe out here," I say.

"Not safe in there, either. You saw how the District comes in and acts like they run the place. I've never seen anyone stand up to them like you did."

I smile, but it's a tired smile. Lilly's sudden appearance irks me more than makes me happy.

"I'm serious. I'm not trying to suck up to you, Jack," she says.

"Thanks," I say.

"What did you do to the one you tied up? Brandon is his name, right?" she asks.

"*Was* his name," I say. The way I speak gives me chills. Heartless monster comes to mind, and I'm not thinking about Brandon. I'm thinking about myself.

"You killed him." This not a question, either. She looks pale in the moonlight, as if the idea of death is as foreign to her as real zombies were once foreign to the world.

"Not exactly," I say, and this is true. I didn't kill Brandon, but I didn't help him, either. Getting out of those ropes wouldn't have been impossible if he had more time. I don't want to think about it anymore. What happened there is something I don't understand, something I don't think I'll ever understand. The way his eyes blanked out and he talked about seeing the future. It was like some sort of voodoo that has no place in the real world.

"I heard the gunshots and the screaming."

"I wasn't screaming," I say. "I don't scream."

Did I? What the hell happened out there?

"I heard someone screaming." She crosses her arms as if I've offended her. Maybe she heard Brandon and I hadn't in my rush to get out of there.

I look over my shoulder across the bridge. I'm guessing we're only about a half-mile away from where all those zombies were. Too close. Much too close.

"Come on," I say. "We gotta get out of here. It's not safe."

I dismount Bilbo. It seems like the gentlemanly thing to do. I could invite her up on the horse to ride him with me, but that seems weird. Seems like I'd be betraying Darlene in some unspeakable way.

"Why'd you follow me?" I ask.

She hesitates, runs a hand through her short, dark hair. Even in the night, her eyes shine. "You intrigued me."

"Intrigued you?"

"Yeah. You're different. You're *good.*"

"Good?" I laugh. "Hardly. There's no such thing as good anymore. Only evil, bad, and gray. I'm closer to bad than I am gray, and there's some days where I feel just plain evil."

"We've all done things we aren't proud of," she says, a hand on the saddle, walking in rhythm with the horse, who snorts at her touch. "It was true before the world ended and it's still true now. But I don't think you've done anything without purpose. You've never done anything purely out of evilness."

I think about that for a moment. "What about

those men I killed back in your bar?" I pause and look at her.

"You did what you did because you didn't want to see Shiv die."

"Shiv?" I ask.

"The piano player."

I did what I did because Brandon and the other guards deserved to die.

We approach a fork in the road. I know if we go west, we'll eventually end up back in Freeland's orbit. I have no intention of going that way, but neither do I have any intention of picking up a partner on this journey of revenge. So I point at the road and hand Lilly the reins.

"Looks like your exit is coming up," I say.

She frowns. Ignores me.

I stop, making sure the horse stops with me, otherwise Lilly is liable to go on. I hate to be the bearer of bad news here, but I'm pretty sure I have to give it to her straight or she'll just follow me around like a lost puppy who thinks I'm its mother.

"Back to Freeland," I say.

She says nothing.

"Or wherever you want to go. Just not with me," I continue.

Still, she says nothing.

Now it's my turn to frown. I hope it comes off more natural than my smiles do.

"You don't know how good you got it there in Freeland," I say. "You're protected."

"By the District? Hardly," she replies. Her arms cross again. It's a gesture I'm beginning to not particularly like.

"Hey, it's better than no protection at all. Like out here." I sweep my hand around the road. It's overgrown. Weeds stick up from the cracks in the asphalt. The lines aren't as faded as they were on the roads I took to get here, but you can tell no city street department has been this way in a *long* time.

"I can handle myself." Lilly moves her long-sleeved shirt up at the waist. On her hip, a big revolver hangs. It's ancient. I think about Norm's *Dirty Harry* gun, about the Colts gunslingers use. I've fired one before. It has a hell of a kickback. In my mind's eye, I see Lilly flung a few feet backwards as she pulls the trigger.

"I suppose if you've survived this long, then you can handle yourself," I say. "But I'm not looking for company."

"Company? What do you think I am, a prostitute?" She smirks at this.

I ignore the remark. "This is my mission and my

mission alone," I say, trying to insert a sense of finality into my voice.

"It doesn't have to be. I hate the District just as much as you do. You ever seen *Star Wars?*" she asks.

"*Me* seen *Star Wars?*" I chuckle. "Of course, I've seen it. Who hasn't?"

"Well, I have, but it's not exactly my favorite movie."

I grimace, all humor going out of me. "*Star Wars* should be everyone's favorite movie. Especially *Empire Strikes Back*. That's my favorite."

"That's the one where Darth Vader says, 'Luke, I am your father,' right?"

"Not exactly what he says, but at least you know that much," I reply. *Star Wars* used to be one of my favorite things. I showed it to Junior. We marathoned all seven main movies and it was beautiful. But now that memory hurts, and instead of seeing the hope in *Star Wars*, I just see the bad. The Empire took over the galaxy, slaughtered the Jedi and scores of people and aliens while they were at it. They were defeated, but evil never dies. It always rises again.

"It was my son's favorite movie, too," I say absentmindedly.

"You have a son?" Lilly asks, her voice hopeful.

"Had a son," I say.

She nods, looks down at her shoes. Understanding. I know that look, it's the polite look of people who think they've overstepped their boundaries or offended you in someway.

"I had a little brother," she says. "And a mom and a dad and a boyfriend."

A silence falls over us. It's near complete in the stillness of the road. All that can be heard is the chirping of bugs, the intermittent coos of birds dream-talking, the snorting breath of Bilbo. I stand up straight. "Anyway, back to *Star Wars*. I feel like you were about to make a point there, or something close to it."

"Right," Lilliana says, nodding. "*Star Wars*. I was going to compare the District to the evil Empire. You know, the big bad people a plucky group of nobodies-turned-to-heroes has to defeat before all hope is entirely lost. Luke couldn't defeat Vader and the Empire by himself. He needed Han and Leia. He needed Chewie, and those cute robots," Lilly continues.

"But they just come back in Episode VII," I say flatly.

She arches an eyebrow. "Didn't see that one."

"Yep, back to Freeland you go," I say. "Let

someone else worry about bringing down the 'Empire'."

"No," she says.

"Why?" I ask. It is a question I seem to be asking more so than usual. "Why me? You don't even know me."

"Because I saw what you're capable of. You may not be a good person—which I doubt—but you certainly know what you're doing when it comes to taking down the District."

"It's not about taking them down," I say. We are still standing at this fork in the road. I am annoyed, frightened, shaken.

"Then what's it about?" Lilly puts her hands on her hips, cocks her head at me. The way she does it reminds me of Abby. She was the little sister I never had, the wise-cracking, know-it-all, who would be there for you no matter what. God, I miss her. God, I miss all of them. The thought of my family, of all who I've lost, makes my answer come out smooth and natural.

"It's about revenge. Simple as that."

"Now we're talking," Lilly says. "What better revenge than bringing them *all* down?"

I look at her sternly. It's hard not to picture her gutted, her organs hanging out, her heart no longer beating. All because of what? She wanted to follow me? I will not have her blood on my hands along with everyone else's.

Then again, Jack...what's a little more blood to add to the mix?

No.

"Go home," I say. "Go back to Freeland. Live out the rest of your life without anymore bloodshed."

"There's always bloodshed."

"It's out of your hands sometimes, yeah, but there's less bloodshed when you don't go out looking for danger."

"I'm not looking for danger," she says.

My eyes go wide, and my arms are out to the side. "What are you talking about? You want to overthrow an entire apocalyptic empire! If that's not danger, then I don't know what is."

She shakes her head.

I hand her Bilbo's reins. The horse is content with standing here, nose to the ground, tail swishing back and forth as sporadically as the hooting of owls in the nearby forests. "Take him back to Bill or Curly. Whatever the hell his name is."

"No," she says, and she actually stamps her foot down. The echo of sole hitting asphalt rolls among the trees.

Don't have time for this.

I'm not giving up. I just choose to end the argument. To the right, I go.

I'm taking the horse with me.

"Wait," she says. There is a slight desperation in her voice. I sense it because I've heard this desperation in my own voice before.

I stop, turn around, and look at her. She knows I can hop onto Bilbo and leave her in a cloud of dust. Will I do that?

Probably not.

They say chivalry died long before everyone else did, but I don't believe that. Who would I be to leave a poor, defenseless woman to the dark? Not to mention the surrounding horde of zombies undoubtedly tracking our scent right now as we speak.

I stare at Lilliana, waiting for her to say her argument, her last desperate attempt.

And she does.

"I have a working car," she says.

I narrow my eyes at her. Impossible. These days, the only cars you see driven are by the higher ranking District officers. Not even Brandon is that —*was* that, my apologies. And these days, I tell it like it is. No other way to do it. "Bullshit."

She raises her right hand. I get a glimpse of that gun she has on her belt again. "Honest to God," she says. "There's one catch, though." She shrugs when she sees my expression.

"Always a catch, huh?" I say.

"It's about twenty miles away and the man who owns it is one tough son of a bitch," she says. "He's got guns—*a lot* of guns—and soldiers willing to die for his cause."

I'm silent for a long moment.

"Jack?" Lilly says in a soft voice that I barely hear, even in all the silence.

I shake my head. I can't believe I'm going to do this. But a car? Jesus Christ, that would make things so much easier.

Safer, too.

"It's a working car, right? Not some piece of shit clunker?" I ask.

Lilliana nods eagerly.

For a moment, I'm transported back to a time where I watched one of the most famous safe havens crumble. Eden. The way we escaped was by stealing a beat-up van. A piece of shit clunker, if you will. That van lasted us longer than it should've. So maybe even a clunker is better than nothing at all.

"It's nice. I've seen it in action many times before," Lilly says.

"Whose is it?"

"An officer's."

"You mean a District officer's?"

She nods, her face going ashy. "He is not a very nice man."

"To become an officer in the District, one cannot be remotely close to nice," I say. I try to picture this man. I'm having trouble, especially with the image of Brandon's neck and face being torn away by chomping zombie teeth so fresh in my mind.

"I was going to steal it myself," she says.

"Why don't you?"

She grins, but she hasn't gotten the color back in her face. "Well," she says, "like I said, Luke was nothing without Han, was he?"

All I can do is shake my head. She just doesn't understand.

10

THE SUN IS COMING UP NOW. TO A MAN LIKE ME, ONE who sleeps the day away and patrols the night because there's less people about, this ungodly hour is hardly dinnertime. We have been taking turns riding Bilbo. Neither of us is comfortable enough to share the horse. I am content with walking.

Lilly is in the saddle, dozing off. I could just leave her right now. I could save any future pain she might cause me. Whether that pain would be inflicted by losing her or by betrayal, time will only tell.

But should I even risk this?

I don't know. The prospect of leaving her seems enticing, if only because it has been so long since I've been in the company of others on the road.

Then again, I have to keep my number one goal

right there where it belongs at the top. That, of course, is revenge. The longer it takes me to get to Ohio, my chances of revenge slip further away. Same goes for ever finding out what happened to my brother and Abby.

Sometimes, I wish I would've found their bodies among the remains of the countless others slaughtered at Haven. At least then I would have known what happened to them. I would've been able to lay them to rest the way I had laid Darlene and Junior to rest.

The unknown is so much worse than the known.

Lilly mumbles something in her sleep. It sounds like *'Momma.'*

My hand finds its way into my inside breast pocket. For a moment, my insides go cold. The pocket is anything but empty. All of my important items are in here, but the most important item seemingly isn't.

That would be the locket, the one that contains the picture of my wife and son, that moment of perfection captured by a Polaroid.

I stop in the road. Bilbo doesn't, and since the broken reins are currently tied around my wrist, Bilbo's force pulls me forward.

"Damn it," I say. "Hold on."

The horse listens.

Lilly stirs in the saddle. She moans sleepily, then this moan turns into a deep yawn. Out of the corner of my eye, I see her stretching. Not for long, though, because I'm ripping my cloak off. The cool, fall air blasts me through my t-shirt, sending chills all up my spine.

"Where is it?" I say, turning my cloak upside down and shaking everything in the pockets free.

"Jack?" Lilly's voice says. "Jack, are you okay?"

Batteries and pill bottles clatter off the road, bouncing up and down, rolling to the ditch. Band-Aids float lazily toward my feet, caught on the morning breeze. There's a pocket knife, well-used, that cartwheels out of my line of sight. Bullets, clips, rifle attachments such as red-dot sights, ACOG scopes, and a homemade silencer that is anything but silent.

Lilly gets off the horse now.

"Jack? You're kinda freaking me out here, man," she says.

"Where is it?" I'm mumbling, my head completely and totally someplace else.

"Where's what?"

Tears are on the verge. I can feel them. I don't want to cry in front of this woman, this stranger, but

I can't help myself. Besides the memories, that picture is all I have left of Darlene and Junior—and my memories are not solid like the picture is; they're fading, fading, fading...

"Is it this?" Lilly says, but I'm almost too lost in this current nightmare to hear her. By some desperation, I look up and see her in the grass off of the side of the road. She holds something small between her thumb and index finger. It glimmers, catches the early sunshine.

Relief floods me.

I spring up, still forgetting that Bilbo's reins are tied to me. Naturally, the horse is heavy and though I'm stronger than I was fifteen years ago, I'm nothing compared to the beast whose hooves are planted firmly on the asphalt. I fall backward, landing on a minefield of batteries, bullets, and every sharp thing in the world.

Should hurt, but the adrenaline is pumping and I hardly feel it. I will later.

Scrambling up, trying to break free of the sliced reins—and I'm so anxious to get the one piece of my old life back I consider ripping my arm off and shambling at this strange woman like a mutilated zombie.

"Don't open—" I shout.

It's too late. Lilly puts her long nail into the crack and the locket glides smoothly open.

I finally get free of Bilbo's reins and I'm running at Lilly faster than I'd run from a horde of the dead. I snatch the locket out of her hands. In my palm, the pendant feels so right. I look at that perfect moment, the picture, and the tears that were on the verge spill over. They ride the lines in my face only to get lost in my beard. I turn away so Lilly doesn't see me cry, but the noises betray me. I'm sniffling, trying to swallow down hitching sobs.

She says nothing. All is still in the countryside except for me. Even Bilbo watches me curiously for a moment before he realizes his leash has been unhooked and he's free to graze on the crabgrass nearby. Which he does greedily.

I want to jump through the photo back to that moment. I want to hug my wife and son one more time before they're gone forever. I have so many regrets. I would've never yelled at Junior. I would've let him watch all the scary movies he wanted to watch despite him being much too young for those types of gory and frightening films. I would've let him stay at his friends and ditch the schooling Laura Harkinson taught the youngsters Monday through Friday. I would never have argued with Darlene. I would take her into my arms and never let her go. I would've told her how beautiful she was every chance I got. I would've read those trashy romance novels she liked so much just so I could talk to her about them into the wee hours of the night. I would've done all of this and more.

But it's too late.

They're gone. Gone for good.

And it's my fault, and all I have left of them is this little rectangular picture, so small I can hardly see the color of Darlene's eyes or my son's gap-toothed smile. What if I forget those things? What if I forget that Darlene's favorite shampoo was strawberry scented, that Junior's last baby tooth was his front one and he didn't lose it until he was accidentally elbowed by his friend Joey while shooting hoops.

I can't take this. I can't take it any longer.

"Jack?" Lilly's voice drifts through the heavy sadness clouding my thoughts. "Jack, are you okay?"

I'm not okay. I'm anything but okay.

"Yeah, I'm fine. Just thought I lost it," I lie.

"Jack, it's okay. I understand," she says. She stands over me now, her hand out and resting on my shoulder. "Here, let me help you." She bends down and begins picking up all the little knick-knacks that were in my cloak.

"Thank you," I say.

After everything is picked up, Lilly reaches back behind her neck and takes her own necklace off. It has a small crucifix on it. She slides the pendant off, her eyes narrowed in concentration as her fingers work. Once the pendant is free, she hands me the chain. It's thin, sterling silver. "Here," she says. "So you don't lose it again."

The chain hangs over her fingers like a strand of a spider's web.

"I think it'll fit," she says.

"No—I can't."

"Jack. Just take it."

"But it's your necklace," I say. "You need it."

She chuckles, holds the small cross up to her eyes. Unlike the chain, I don't believe the pendant is real. It looks cheaply made. Of course, I know that doesn't matter if it's important to her. Importance is all about perspective, not how much something's worth.

"I'm not even religious," she says. "This cross—I only wear it because I thought it was cool."

"That's reason enough to keep it," I say, but I can see plainly on her face that she doesn't believe me.

"Like I said," she continues, ignoring me, "I'm not religious. Not anymore, anyway." She spins around, sweeping her hands out to the landscape. "Once I believed in God and Jesus Christ and the Bible and all that stuff, but—" She points to a nearby house up the road. There, a dilapidated fence and overgrown grass and dead crops stare back at us. "But what kind of God would let this happen to the world?"

I say nothing, only look at her with a mixture of contempt and admiration. She is growing on me, and I don't like that. I'm a lone warrior. No more partners, no more people who'll just die—

"Really, I'm not," Lilly says, knocking me off my line of thought. "Plus, there's more crucifixes than there are zombies. That's a guess. Not a fact." She smiles and takes the cross into her closed fist, cocks her arm back, and launches the pendant as far as she can throw it. My jaw drops as I follow its trajectory. For a long moment, it hangs in the air. A shard of silver against the orange sky. Then I lose sight of it. It lands somewhere among the weeds, lost forever.

I turn to face Lilly. She holds the chain out to me again.

"Believe me now?" she asks.

Still, I'm hesitant to take it.

She rolls her eyes and tosses it at me. My natural reaction is to catch it. I do.

Not outwardly happy, I thread the chain through the pendant. The length of the chain is longer than the one it was on before, but I don't care. When I clasp the necklace, I look down and see the pendant is closer to my heart than it was before.

And that just feels right, but I remind myself not to get attached to this woman, not to let her become a friend.

We are back to walking again. Neither of us are on Bilbo. Lilly suggested that the horse needed a break, too, and I agreed with her. I still don't know how I feel having her on this journey with me. We've only been traveling for about half a day, largely in silence.

And I don't like the silence because all I can do is think about Darlene and Junior. So I break it.

"A car," I say.

"Yep," Lilly says.

"I haven't seen a car in two years," I say.

"Not many around here. Where were you two years ago?" she asks, honest curiosity in her voice.

I know if I take too long to answer her question,

she'll know I'm coming up with a lie. I'm not the best at lying.

So I answer Lilly honestly.

"Haven," I say.

Lilly stops walking, and Bilbo does with her.

Before I look at Lilly I already know what her face will look like. Her eyes as wide and round as the noon sun is above our heads. Her fingers touching either her chest, unconsciously clutching the cotton over her heart, or the same fingers resting on her parted lips.

Sure enough, as I turn, I'm wrong.

Instead of a look of surprise, I'd say she looks to be filled with contempt, as if I've somehow insulted her by mentioning Haven. Her arms are crossed over her breasts and she rolls her eyes as she says, "Haven? Okay, Jack. Funny."

"What?" I say.

"You expect me to believe that you were all the way up in San Francisco at one of the best—if not *the* best—communities left in America and you somehow traveled by foot across all these states without a scratch to show for it?"

My heart breaks a little more. She's right. Haven was the best. I made damn sure of it. Along with the help of so many wonderful people, people willing to sacrifice so many amenities for the greater good of the community, we made Haven great. Others came from all over the world to seek out that stretch of land, to have a chance at being helped or even *saved*. And Lilly is also right in thinking this task of travel is impossible. I do, however, have a little more than a few scratches to show for it.

I nod. "Yes, I expect you to believe that because it's the truth."

"There's no way," she says.

I shrug and turn away from her, fingering the locket beneath my cloak. By the grace of the God I may or may not believe in, Bilbo follows me. This way, I don't look like a total ass-hat.

"Is that your wife and son?" Lilly's voice calls after me. "The people in that picture."

I turn around and look at her.

She reads my expression and quickly apologizes. "I know it's not my place," she says. "But I figured if we are going to have a successful partnership, we should probably get to know each other a little better."

I shake my head. "Not necessary."

"Jack, I know you're afraid."

"I'm not afraid," I reply.

"Yes, you are. Everyone left is afraid. If they're not

then they're crazy," she says. "I'm afraid, you're afraid... Even Bilbo here is afraid. It's not a big deal."

I don't answer. I just stare, mentally regretting my decision to let her come around. I'm sure I would come across a working car eventually.

"I had a kid. A baby," Lilly says. Her mouth turns downward.

"I'm sorry," I say.

"Don't be. It happened. It *happens*. Her name was going to be Jean, after my grandmother. The poor old woman practically raised me. My mom worked a lot. Dumped me off at Nana's house." A lone tear streaks down Lilly's face. She absentmindedly wipes it away.

"What happened to Jean?" I find myself asking, though I can guess. Again, after the words have left my lips, I wish I could take them back. Can't get attached.

"Well, Jean was born but not normal..."

I raise my hand to tell her to stop, but she doesn't. I don't want to hear this. There's already enough sadness in this world.

"Jean was infected. The doctor where I was staying was eighty-percent sure that it wouldn't happen. We liked our chances. But I guess the odds weren't in my favor. Doctor Jinkton was actually a veterinarian, so you know, can't blame him. Besides, if I knew she would've been born the way she was born, what would I have done? It's not like we had the tools or knowledge for abortion and it's not like I even believe in that." Another tears streaks down her cheek. She doesn't wipe this one away. "Alas, Jean was born and just as soon as she took a breath…she died and *turned*."

It's like a lightning bolt strikes me right then and there. Anger and sadness burn through the very core of my being. How can life be so unfair? I think back to Junior's own birth, the feeling of dread I had in the pit of my stomach when the doctor and the two nurses held him in their arms. We were in one of the public restrooms Eve had converted into an infirmary. Knocked down the walls separating the men's from the women's, cleaned the hell out of the place, put in hospital beds, and it really did remind me of an honest-to-God infirmary when it was all said and done.

I remember the doctor and the nurse laughing. The clapping. Then them handing me my son for the first time. A beautiful and healthy baby boy. I almost fainted.

"I guess I always knew that what happened *could* happen. God knows they reminded me about it every chance they got. *'Don't get your hopes up, Lilly.' 'Whatever happens, happens for a reason.'* Bullshit," Lilly says.

"I'm sorry," I say again, and I do mean it.

She waves my sorry away. "It was a long time ago. I'm okay. Sure, I carried Jean around for nine months, but I should've it, you know? At some point I felt something...*off* inside of my womb—and I should've known then. But, like a fool, I held out hope. I was more mad than anything."

I nod. I understand. When I found Junior's body lying next to Darlene's, the pool of blood around them, so much that the ground was stained red and the grass was soggy with it, and the initial shock wore off, I was angry. So mad that I was prepared to run to the ends of the earth to find the man who did it. It was only after I buried them that I think I realized that they were gone, gone forever.

Lilly looks out over the horizon, at that dilapidated fence and the equally shabby farmhouse beyond it, which we are directly in front of. I follow her eyes, and for the first time, I realize there is a silo jutting over the house's caved in roof. There might be some sort of grain or feed there we can give to Bilbo. It's a long shot, but looking at the farm and judging by the height of the grass and the land, whoever owned that farm did not die fifteen years ago. It's only recently been vacated, if at all.

I look back to Lilly, see the sadness in her eyes. But I see something else, too. I see understanding. She turns and those knowing eyes meet mine. I hesitate.

I have my own stories of loss to tell. In my head, I know them all too intimately. I've never spoken them out loud, and I think I've never done that because doing so would make them real—somehow realer than they already are.

Right now, after Lilly has told me her own tragic tale, I think it would be unfair of me to withhold mine.

"Yeah, this is my wife and son. Darlene and Herbert Jr.," I say, holding the locket up.

Lilly nods. A smile replaces the frown on her face.

"They were in Haven with me. We helped build it up to what it was. Then the District came and they murdered everyone. Well, mostly everyone. Darlene and Junior were among those. I saw them die. I saw Darlene's throat slit and my own son shot in the back of the head. They left me alive. I'm not sure why. Maybe they thought I was dead. I had blacked out. I don't remember why, could've been from shock or from a blow to the head. When I woke up, I witnessed the aftermath of all the destruction and death firsthand. I held my son's bloody corpse to my chest then I held my wife's, then I held them together. Darlene's head lolled. They had cut her so deep that I could see her vertebrae." I'm not crying. I'm too numb to cry.

Lilly nods, walks over to me, and wraps me up in a hug.

"I'm sorry," she says.

We part.

"This explains a lot," she says now, wiping her tears away. Despite all the sadness, all the heaviness, she smiles.

Confused, I ask, "What do you mean?"

"Why you're such a badass," she says.

"I'm not."

"Don't sell yourself short, Jack. I know I said it earlier...but I've never seen anyone stand up to the District like you did."

"Oh, that's just the beginning. I know where the man who murdered my family is. I won't stop until he's dead," I say and I mean this. I will stop at *nothing* until I succeed. Even if it takes coming back as a zombie and ripping his other eye out.

"That where you're heading?" she asks.

I nod.

"Then that's where I'm heading, too," she says.

I don't want this. I don't want to put her in danger, but I keep silent, thinking that I'll cross that bridge when I get to it.

Despite the overwhelming bad feeling I get when I hop over the fence and onto the field, I don't stop and come back. Emptying my cloak has been eye-opening. I'm down on my last leg of supplies. Now that I have a means of transportation in Bilbo, I can carry more essentials and not be weighted down.

The only problem here is that Bilbo is another life to take care of besides my own. As much as I don't know about horses, I'm not stupid enough to not know that they eat, drink, and sleep just like us humans.

So hopping the fence is for me as much as it's for the horse. Not because I'm getting attached to him. I can't let that happen. It's because if he's going to help me achieve my goal he'll need to be at full strength.

Once in the tall grass and weeds, I crouch low and pull out a pair of binoculars. Scanning the back of the farmhouse, I see nothing, no movement. The back door is cracked open. A couple windows are busted out. Any sane person would not leave these matters unattended. My guess: zombies somehow got in and had a feast and then moved on like the buzzards they are.

I look back to Lilly and the horse. They are hidden in the shadow of a tall tree, a few feet away from the fence. My goal is to scan the area for danger before I give her the go-ahead.

And yes, I thought about her hopping on to Bilbo's back and making off with my horse, leaving me in the middle of nowhere. But I truly don't think she'd do that, and if she did, it's not a big deal. Two less mouths to feed.

I crouch-walk to the silo. It's by no means a big silo, not like the type I've seen in Ohio, the silos that tower over the horizon like mountain peaks, that can be seen a few towns over, filled to the very top with feed and grain.

Inside, I shine a flashlight. The batteries need changed; it takes those fat C or D batteries, and I can't seem to find those anywhere these days. Just as the light burns out, I see two fifty pound bags marked Feed. Horse feed? Maybe, maybe not, but we'll find out if Bilbo's hungry enough to eat it. One of the bags is opened and rolled down. There are barrels of grain behind this and some shovels and other tools propped up on the walls near them. But the feed. How lucky can we get? Finally, something seems to go right for me. I walk over to the full bag and try to lift it. It's heavy, heavier than fifty pounds, I think. No way I'll be able to drag both out by myself. Well, I probably can, but I'll admit that the darkness inside, combined with the old smell of dirt and wood, is starting to get to me. So I go out into the light and wave Lilly and Bilbo inside.

The fence creaks with the sound of rusty hinges opening. They come up a gravel driveway that cuts through the entire property.

It is now that Lilly screams out and falls. I don't know what happens. Now I see her; now I don't. Bilbo rises on hind legs, neighing. Then he takes off, moving faster than I've seen him move.

"Lilly!" I shout. My guts have turned to jelly. I'm thinking the worst as I run toward the spot where Lilly has fallen, where her screams are coming from. Darlene comes to the front of my mind. How many times had I ran after her because of the screams on our way to Haven? Too many times. This is why I wanted to take this journey alone.

The grass rustles and the sound of hands beating the ground fills my ears. Lilly wrestles with a zombie. It is only the torso of a man. The guts and meaty tubes hang out a little farther than the knob of his spinal cord. He has no hair and a drooping tribal tattoo that was once on his upper back obscured with dirt and dry blood.

I plunge into the tangle of limbs and try to pull the zombie off of her, but it's strong. The chance of a hot meal always makes them work harder.

My hand closes around cold, dirty skin. I pull with all my might, but my fingers slip off of whatever part of this dead man I've grabbed, and I fall backward on my ass with a bone-jolting thump.

"Fuck," I mumble.

The zombie growls and roars and gnashes rotten teeth. Lilly no longer screams out of fear. As I scramble to my feet, I see her on her knees, fending off the rabid monster with her forearm and raising her right arm high above her head. In it, she holds a rock no bigger than a fist. She thrusts it downward.

I put my own arms up to shield my face from the spray of blood. The zombie's head caves in with a sickening crunch. All it took was one hit, but Lilly continues to hit it, and hit it, and hit it. Until all that's left of this zombie looks like a large, chewed piece of watermelon gum attached to a bloody neck.

"I can handle myself," Lilly says.

"I wasn't much help anyway," I say. Walking over to her, I offer her my hand. She looks at it like it's some alien object. Then I look at her own hand, seeing how it's covered in blood and brains and tiny dots of white skull, then pull my hand back.

"Gotta get your hands dirty sometimes," Lilly says.

I grimace. "Doesn't mean I like to." I still help her up, but avoid her hands and offer her the crook of my arm.

"Where's Bilbo?" she asks when she's standing.

"Ran," I say. I scan the horizon. I'm tall yet it's still hard for me to see over the rises in the land. I catch a hint of his dark mane near the silo. "Looks like he's found the food. I hope it's all right for him."

"It's fine. A little expired feed never hurt anyone," Lilly says. She swipes drops of blood off of her face. The way she says it, I'm not sure she really means it. I've personally found some expired food and not felt my best after I ate it. I'm a sucker for Reese's Cups... even ones fifteen years past their expiration date that are essentially nothing but chocolatey dust. Still, I suppose expired feed *is* better than nothing for Bilbo.

Probably.

We go to the silo and set it up so he can just eat

out of the bag. He seems to grimace at the taste of it at first but warms up enough to empty the first bag in what is quite possibly record time. Lilly opens the second bag and says, "Might as well eat up. We still got a ways to go."

She's changed since her encounter with the zombie near the gate. She seems…guarded, overtly cautious. I can't blame her, but I wonder if it's because she's been sheltered in Freeland for however long without the dangers of zombies lurking around every corner.

But the thought of her striking the zombie again and again makes me shiver beneath my cloak in the hot sun.

Bilbo continues eating. He doesn't polish off the last bag, though, and judging by the expression on his face, he doesn't particularly like the taste of expired feed. I doubt there's much in the way of nutrients, but it has to be better than eating grass, right? I don't know, I'm not a horse.

We sit in silence, the shadow of the silo stretching over us. It's a hot fall day, hotter than it has any right to be. It's in this silence that my stomach begins to growl; so far, I've learned to ignore this as well as the pangs of hunger constant in the apocalypse, but then I realize it's been nearly twenty-four hours since I've had anything to eat. I think the last bit of sustenance I've had besides a few nips from my water skin is the whiskey I drank at the bar before everything turned to hell with Brandon and his District goons.

My stomach rumbles again. Absentmindedly, my hand clenches it beneath my cloak. Lilly is looking at me out of the corner of her eyes. She is in the light now, the sun basking her, streaking her short, dark hair with oranges and yellows.

My stomach ripples once more, and this time, I can hardly take the pain. I stand up and walk over to the saddle, where my cloak rests. Bilbo is not tethered to anything. I figured he deserved a break as much as we did. He seems to enjoy the sun warming his skin beneath all that shiny hair, but he's as tired as the rest of us and doesn't venture far. He's always only a few feet away, staying away from the taller grass because he can smell the blood of the zombie Lilly crushed. After that incident, I did my best to scan the field for more. I didn't find anything besides the zombie's lower half that was still somehow twitching like a dog in the midst of a nightmare. It was by a well all but hidden in the grass. The stench coming up from the deep darkness was abysmal, so I covered it. No need for one of us to accidentally fall in and break our leg. Actually, I think the smell would kill you before you realized you've even broken your leg.

From my cloak, I take out a wrapped package of cheese. It's homemade stuff I bought at a different outpost about two weeks before I came upon Freeland. It tastes like a boot and smells even worse, but my hunger wins out.

I turn around to offer a piece to Lilly, knowing she'll probably refuse because she's used to better eating in Freeland, but as my eyes search for hers, I see that she's sleeping. Out cold.

I sit down against the cool stone of the silo and rest my head. The idea of sleep is nice, but I know I can't doze off right now. I'll stay up for another hour, maybe two, then I'll wake Lilly. We have to keep watch over one another. If we don't, the next time we wake up a couple zombies might be chewing on our insides. Or we might not wake up at all, at least not as humans.

I eat as much of the cheese as I can stomach before its sour taste is too much to bear. Besides, I need to save it for later. Who knows how long it'll be before we discover food?

Who knows—

An idea comes to mind, one that is slow to hit me because of the exhaustion I'm suffering from.

I go over to Lilly and rouse her awake. She moans, "What?"

"I'm going up to the house, take a look around. Can you go in the silo until I come back?" I ask. I won't be able to watch her while I'm inside even though I don't think I'll be inside for long.

"Yeah," she says sleepily. Then she opens her eyes fully and it seems like she's been wide awake this whole time. In her normal, not sleep-heavy voice, she says, "You better not leave me, Jack. If you do, I'll find you."

"Don't worry. I won't leave you until I get some sleep." Plus, I need to know where that car is and Lilly is the one leading me.

She smiles and closes her eyes again as I help her up and guide her to the silo. Inside, it's cool and dark, the perfect place to sleep on this warm day. Bilbo comes inside, too, sniffs around curiously at the feed bags, one empty and the other half-full. Now that he's here, I decide to shut him in with Lilly, too. Better safe than sorry, I suppose. He doesn't care much. He's not like a dog that'll whine and bark and draw attention to us. I'm grateful for that. Not to mention that Lilly won't be in there alone.

As I make my way up to the farmhouse, I feel pretty awake. It's the thrill of the mission that reenergizes me. I've always hated scouting abandoned buildings because you never know exactly what you'll find; you just know it's usually not going to be anything good.

There are tire tracks in the gravel, thick ones left from a tractor, I think. I don't know how long ago, but if they're still there, I think it hasn't been as long as I originally thought. My hand goes to the sword on my back. No. That won't do. I pull my pistol out of its holster. Again, better safe than sorry.

The front porch creaks beneath my weight. The wood is old and moldy. I smell mildew and rot. At the door, I tap the butt of my gun against the wood three times. A few chips of red paint, like dry blood, flake off and drift down to my boots.

My heartbeat is surprisingly calm, but an iciness has begun to course through my body. It's anticipation. It's fear.

I hit the door to alert any zombies inside. Wait a few moments. Nothing happens, nothing comes. Still not knowing if entering is safe or not, I push the door open anyway. It creaks loudly, the noise echoing in the vast emptiness.

I take a step forward.

The inside of the farmhouse is covered in blood. It hasn't even gotten the chance to dry yet.

The hall runner squishes beneath my feet. It is red, but I don't think it was originally that color. Bloody handprints smear and streak the drywall. Some of the frames that once hung in the hall are on the floor, face down. Others are still hanging crookedly. Pictures of a happy family near a lighthouse, near a beach, graduation photos, piano recitals, high school basketball team photos. I don't study these closely. There's no need to because the people in these photos are gone, long gone. I remember back to a time when I entered an abandoned house with Darlene, Norm, and Abby. There were pictures just like these sitting on the living room mantle, pictures I picked up and looked at. The feeling that invaded me then was one of sadness, of dread. I don't need more of that in my life.

So I avoid the pictures and walk down the blood-soaked runner. At the end of the corridor, on my left, a staircase winds up to the second floor. An old suit of armor stands guard near the railing and the first step. It's dusty, dented, as if it has seen many battles. I pause and run my hand over the helmet. Grittiness comes off, sticks to my finger tips. This could be useful, I'm thinking, then chuckle at the idea of me riding around on a horse in a suit of medieval armor. If that ever becomes a reality, the world is *truly* over.

Around the staircase and through another door, I see a bathroom. A smear of blood greases the hardwood, hardly visible in the low light. Through this door, the hardwood ends only to be taken over by carpet. The carpet, originally white, is now pink. Streaks of blood here, streaks of blood there. The television is big, but it's busted and glass is embedded into the floor. I step around it, scanning for more signs of blood. Of course, there is, and my pulse quickens. With anticipation? With fear? I have no clue. All I do know is that I'm drawn to the gore, to the macabre. The need to know what happened here on this farm weighs heavy on my mind. I know I won't be able to search the house for supplies without knowing for sure that no monsters are lurking around the corner.

But these days, it seems monsters are *always* lurking around the corner.

Through this family room I go. I guess there's not much of a family left here, but oh well. Two windows are on each side of the television. Covering the glass are bags of sand, like it's a war zone.

Now on the threshold of the kitchen and dining

room, I catch a smell. My nose must be used to this particular stench because I don't smell it until I'm near the dinner table.

To my left, the smell is coming from a dark hallway. I'm nearer the front of the house now. There's a bathroom in this corridor, but the door's closed. I reach for the doorknob, feel something crusty caked to it. Pulling my hand away from the brass and leaning back into the light in the dining room, I see red flakes.

Blood.

Probably against my better judgment, I continue on. The bathroom door opens soundlessly. I hold my breath and raise my gun, ready to put a bullet into the brains of anything that moves.

Nothing.

It's empty except for a sink and a toilet and a small hand towel hanging on a rack between the two. There aren't even signs of blood inside. Whoever was trying to make it here must not have had the strength to turn the knob.

I turn away from the bathroom and plunge down into the darkness. A door on my left. I open it and look inside. It's the garage. There's a car inside—a Ford truck, extremely old. The idea of trying it to see if it works crosses my mind, and I'm halfway down the two concrete steps that lead to the garage floor when I see that there's a mess of pipes and wires and rusty metal hanging out from beneath it, as if some giant beast has gouged the underside with even bigger, killer claws. There's some tools around the other side, socket wrenches, pliers, an entire tool box. Whoever was here before us was trying to fix it up. Without much luck, it seems.

I turn around and go back into the house.

Around this last corner, there is one room. Beneath the smell of death and rot, there is something I haven't smelled in a long time. It's Hawaiian Breeze, it's Downy.

This is a laundry room. If I could just hold onto the smell of freshly washed clothes for a little longer, I'd be the happiest man in the world, but I can't.

Death wins out, like it always does in the end.

The door is cracked. The crack isn't wide enough for me to stick more than the muzzle of my pistol inside. As I lean closer, the mixing scents of death and detergent blast me.

It's too dark inside to see what lurks inside. There's no sound, though, and that's good.

Fear is trying to paralyze me. I don't let it.

I am the Jack Jupiter that has lost everything, who has nothing else to lose. Nothing to fear. Right?

I take a deep breath, and instantly regret it as that terrible smell finds its way onto my taste buds and for the smallest of moments, I can actually taste the death.

I push the door open. It creaks on old hinges just as the front door had earlier. As if this couldn't get any more creepier. Gray light from this hallway I stand in floods into the laundry room, painting the blood on the walls with an eerie glow.

And there's *a lot* of blood on the walls.

It sprays upward in a starburst of red. Drops have congealed on the ceiling, hanging there, waiting for the right amount of vibration or heat to make them fall. I have to put a hand over my mouth and stifle the gagging.

Flies buzz around as the door moves. Maggots squirm over a sunken in face.

I am looking at a corpse. Not a zombie. The corpse of a woman. Her hair was once gray, I think, but the old blood stuck to the stringy strands has turned it nearly black. I can see exposed brains from a hole in her head. It's a bullet wound, and I would know this even if she wasn't holding a shotgun in two pale-gray hands connected to arms so frail that you wouldn't think an old woman like this would be able to lift the weapon high enough to hit herself in the head in the first place.

But she did, and here I am dealing with the aftermath.

Well, there it is, mystery uncovered. On her arm is a bite mark. I'm guessing from the half-zombie Lilly bashed to a second-death. Probably a son or a grandson who got bit and decided to take a bite out of granny. Granny couldn't live with the fact of coming back as a monster so she put a bullet in her own brain.

Case closed.

I search the rest of the house. Don't find much of anything useful. Some Spam, a few cans of vegetables, and some hydrogen peroxide. I take it all.

Better than nothing.

11

When I go outside, the first thing I hear is the splintering of wood. A spike of alarm jolts my tiredness away. On the far side of the field, a group of zombies have gathered, moaning, groaning, pushing up against the fence. The fence is cracking.

I rush to Lilly and wake her up. She jumps to her feet, already knowing the drill. I'm thankful for that.

"I'll grab the stuff," she says and darts into the silo, disappearing amongst the shadows.

I'm doing my best to try to calm the horse down, who has now noticed the zombies traversing through the tall grass. Once my hand brushes his mane, that seems to do some good and he stops bucking.

"Lilly!" I shout. Time is short. The zombies are

halfway across the field, like a sea of disease and chaos. Fear tightens my chest and I'm realizing Bilbo is calming me down as much as I'm calming him down.

"Coming," Lilly calls back. She bursts through the doors of the silo holding her bag and Bilbo's gear. "I'll saddle him up."

I point to the wave of zombies. "No time." I say. "Just have to outrun them far enough to gain some ground." This is no time to panic. I've taken part in this rodeo many times before. A horde of zombies is nothing new. It's times like these that I'm grateful for them being the slower type, and not the freaking sprinting zombies that were popular in living dead flicks in the early 2000s. If that were the case, I don't think there'd be a human left alive on this planet. We'd all either be in some zombie's stomach or zombies ourselves.

Lilly points to the back gate we'd entered in. I shake my head. The back gate is compromised. Right now, the zombies haven't passed it, but by the time we get to it, we'll be on a collision course with death.

"Then what?" she asks, her voice urgent. I take my bag and sling it over my shoulder. Then I put Bilbo's reins around him like a dog leash. He's not particularly fond of this, but we don't have the option to do it the right way.

"Sorry," I say.

He whinnies and his eyes bolt to the side to get a better look at the zombies. Closer now. Always closer now. I can smell the pungent scent of their disease.

"Hold this," I say to Lilly and hand her the reins. I unholster my revolver, cock it, and shoot at the fence. Then one more time, aiming at the bottom piece, weakening it. I kick out with my bloody boots and make a hole big enough for Bilbo to squeeze through.

Lilly shoots once behind me. Unfortunately, I turn around in time to see the face of a too-young-to-die-zombie evaporate into a mess of pink and white and black. It drops headless and trips up a few of its buddies.

Now we're running, Bilbo trotting along with us, keeping pace, the wind whipping his mane back. I risk a glance over my shoulder and see the wave of zombies get tripped up by the fence. Some fall and spear themselves on jagged pieces of wood.

Good riddance, I think to myself.

As we approach a tree just off the side of the road, Lilly and I bend over, hands on our knees, catching our breath. She looks up at me and laughs like a lunatic. I can only stare at her cross-eyed, confused. This is no laughing matter.

"What?" I say, winded.

"What. A. Rush!" she shouts, shaking her head.

I'm slightly pissed off she's not taking this seriously, I say nothing and begin to saddle Bilbo up. I've never done this before and it shows. After about two minutes of embarrassing myself, Lilly sighs and says, "Here, let me help."

I let her, watching her as she does it. It's as confusing as I thought it would be. It doesn't matter as long as it gets done.

"Go ahead," I say, motioning to Bilbo's saddle. "I'll walk."

Lilly shakes her head. "No way, Jack. I got some sleep in the silo. You didn't. About time you did."

Taking another glance over my shoulder, I see the zombies behind us. They're a small black cloud against the backdrop of the sky, but they won't stay that way.

They'll keep coming. They always do.

Until then, I guess some sleep would do me good.

12

Rough hands jolt me awake.

"How much farther do we have to go?" I ask, sleepily. The sun is closer to setting. I've slept longer than intended, but I needed it. I really needed it.

My hand comes to the locket around my neck.

She points past my shoulder. On the horizon, is a forest of trees bisected by a curving road. Past the trees, a large windmill—that looks minuscule to us from here—turns lazily with the breeze. Through the trees is a few acres of farmland, the fields are perfectly neat, plowed or harvested—not sure what the correct term is. Something moves within one. It looks like a small vehicle, but from this distance, I can't exactly tell.

"That's where we're going," Lilly says.

I take out a pair of binoculars and look at the place. Many people are walking about, people who walk with a purpose. Busy worker bees. Almost all of them have guns. I see a black vehicle moving away from us toward a red barn. With the binoculars I can plainly see that its a tractor. The only thing off about it is that I can't hear it—and in this quiet countryside, you can hear damn near anything. I can't see any exhaust coming out of its exhaust pipe, either.

This gives me a bad feeling. My logic tells me that it's safe to assume a place with a working car would also be able to have a working tractor.

For now, I put it to the back of my mind. Working car or not, we are heading to one of the places run by a high-ranking District officer. This means there's a chance of finding out more information about the one-eyed man and what became of Norm and Abby.

At worst, the car turns out to be a dud.

At best, it doesn't.

Either way, I'm killing every District soldier in this place.

13

We're closer now, and what I see disgusts me. The answer to the riddle of the moving tractor not giving off exhaust or making noise presents itself. I look through the binoculars and shake my head.

"What?" Lilly says. I hand them to her. "Poor bastards," she says and hands them back. "But what did you expect?"

I take another look. Part of me thinks I might recognize the prisoners currently attached to the front of the tractor, acting as the engine. Maybe it's Norm or Abby or Tim or Carmen. I know that won't be the case. If it was Tim or Carmen, I would probably scream. They're dead. I buried their bodies myself in a shallow mass grave. If I had more time, I would've buried them one by one, their own plot, headstone, flowers—the works. But the border was compromised by the zombies and there was no telling how long I had before the District came back. I thought of waiting, of sticking it out. Maybe the one-eyed man would come back. I mean, who would be crazy enough to pass up the land Haven was on? Aside from a few broken fences and walls, this place went untouched for the better part of thirteen years.

Like Brandon said, it wasn't about land or safety or expanding the District's borders. No. It was completely about domination, about destruction, about sending a message. The one-eyed man just wanted to torture us, to show he was better.

But he made a big mistake. He left me alive and I'm so close to catching him that I can practically smell his festering, empty eye socket.

The men and women dragging the tractor along wear harnesses. Attached to these harnesses are sticks for them to bite down on. I'm guessing it's to curb their screaming. Now that we're closer, I realize I can't hear their screams. I wonder if they even have enough energy left in them to scream or cry. They are ragged, as emaciated as the oldest zombies. Their skin is riddled with wounds and pockmarks, bright red slashes across their backs. Behind them, in between the grille of the tractor and themselves, is a group of zombies. They are only a few feet behind these poor souls, their arms outstretched. If one of the people slip up and fall, they have about three seconds to get back up before they become zombie chow, and I'm betting these zombies haven't had their jaws and claws removed.

I shake my head and hand the binoculars back to Lilly. A large rock in the nearby woods is our cover. Bilbo is currently tethered to the trunk of an oak in a copse of trees. No one could see him through all the branches, not even me and I'm about fifteen feet away. I can hear his soft whinnies and slow chomping. Apparently the expired horse feed didn't fill him up nearly as much as I expected. The saying *'You eat like a horse'* makes a lot more sense to me.

"There he is!" Lilly shouts, her voice entirely too loud. "Right there!"

I shush her and pull us both down behind the rock, afraid our noise will carry on the wind. Velvety moss tickles the back of my neck.

"That's the guy. They call him Bandit," Lilly is saying.

"Bandit? What a dumb name," I whisper.

"*Okay,* Jack *Jupiter,*" Lilly says and snickers.

I sigh. I've been doing that a lot since I've met

Lilly. She's annoying, but I'll admit...she has proven to be useful.

"Like I have room to talk," Lilly mumbles.

"Huh?"

"My name is Lilliana Wildflower. Did I ever tell you my last name? I don't think I did. It's not like it really matters anymore. I'm surprised I remember it. I've forgotten so many things. My social security number, my old addresses, schoolteachers I had. All of that seems like another life ago." She's still whispering, but I wish she'd just be quiet. I'm trying to listen to the wind and her voice rattles around my head.

I put my hand on her arm and this surprises her enough to quiet her rambling. It's unexpected by both parties. Been awhile since I've shown any sign of gentleness. Mostly because it's been me, myself, and I. Really, I'm not trying to be gentle; I'm just trying to find a more effective way to get this woman to shut up.

Slowly, I poke my head up over the rock, looking through the binoculars. Nothing has changed at the farm. Prisoners are still running from the zombies which is pulling the tractors and the plow behind it. A man sits in the tractor's cabin, smoking a cigarette and smiling big. He has sunglasses on.

"Where is he?" I ask.

"Older guy near the house. He was standing with another fella with bright red hair," Lilly answers.

I scan the horizon. I see the guy with the bright red hair. He can't be much older than Lilly. His shirt is off and he has a cringe-worthy tattoo of a crucifix over his heart. It's not the content of the tattoo that makes me cringe, but rather the design. It's like he got drunk and did it himself, shaky lines, mismatched lengths and all. If one was to go to hell for a tattoo, it would be this one.

"Don't see him—" I begin to say just as something gets my attention. It's the garage door rising, off to the side of the house. I focus my binoculars there, turning the wheel in the middle to adjust the sight. Sure enough, there's a car. The taillights flare up red and the exhaust pipe spits out a fresh cloud of smoke. I'm nearly giddy with excitement. A car. A real, working car.

We can faintly hear the rumble of its engine from our vantage point.

Lilly is going, "Mmm, mmm, mmm. Told ya."

Thank God. A car. A real fucking car.

"I'm very grateful for you, Lilly Wildflower," I say, and this momentary slip of kindness is like the old

Jack Jupiter, the one who died with Darlene and Junior.

She rolls her eyes and punches me a little too hard. I'm taken to the past, thinking of Abby Cage and how she'd punch Norm and I the same way if we said something stupid or annoyed her—which happened quite often now that I think about it. A deep, paling sadness invades my chest and the smiling I had been doing vanishes. A car cannot fix the hole in my heart.

Back to business, I think, wondering where this man named Bandit is going on this fine day. Then I realize it doesn't matter, we'll wait for him and his precious vehicle, no matter what.

But he goes nowhere except out of the garage, backing up near the side of the house, clearing the driveway.

Also curious.

"What's going on?" Lilly asks. She pokes her head up next to mine, squinting her eyes. I hand her the binoculars.

"Hell if I know. He moved the car out of the garage," I say.

"Maybe it's because he wants us to come steal it. You know, making it easier for us."

"Doubt that," I say.

Lilly shrugs. "It's not a bad thing to hope, Jack."

I ignore this. Yes, it is a bad thing to hope. Hope leads to disappointment, and this world is nothing but disappointment.

Coming from behind us, a sound like a jet engine. Fear spikes through me, raising my blood pressure and causing my heart to feel like it's going to burst out of my chest. I'm so caught up in surveying this farm, I forget about any other threats.

My hand goes to my gun, but Lilly already has hers drawn and aiming at the road.

Then it comes, what the sound is. It's a truck, one of those big-ass semis that always used to take up the highway, I think. I look out over the road and see that it's not exactly as big as I remembered. It's more like a U-Haul truck—in fact, it is a U-Haul truck—but in this silence, a cat's meow could be mistaken for a lion's roar.

Another spike of fear ripples through me. "Shit. The horse," I say. I get up to try to move Bilbo out of the view of the road, but Lilly's hand clamps down on my arm and throws me back to my haunches.

"No time," she says. "Just gotta hope."

Hope. Enough about hope.

I'm not hoping anymore and never will *hope* again.

The sound drives Bilbo to whinny much too loudly. If I could just get over there to calm him, maybe even wrap him and wrestle him to the forest floor like the cowboys used to do in my favorite Western movies when they were hiding from outlaws or Indians, then it'd be okay.

No time. Lilly won't even let me. Her hand is still clamped on my forearm. I try my best to make myself as invisible as possible, blended in with the rock, but it's not an easy task.

Sure enough, as the truck approaches, it slows. The hydraulic hiss of its brakes are like death's cold breath on the back of my neck. The hair there prickles and my shirt and cloak shake with my thudding heartbeat. I pick up the shotgun that was leaning on the mossy boulder.

They've stopped.

Damn it all to hell.

The driver's side door opens. I can make out a thin man in overalls wearing a well-worn White Sox cap and the front of the truck. It's orange and white. The windshield is cracked.

"That a fuckin horse?" this guys says, and he talks like he's got something clenched between his teeth. I see a puff of smoke. The wind catches it and brings the smell of burning tobacco in my direction.

Now the passenger's door opens and a skinny black man slams it shut.

"No way," the black man says.

"Hell yes, it is," the driver says. He fumbles at his belt as he tries to free his gun. The sure sign of someone whose been protected by others rather than protecting himself. "Imagine how much jerky we can make from this beaut, Duane. Mmm. Been awhile since I've had horse meat. Hell, been awhile since I've had any meat."

"Put that shit away, you dumbass," the man named Duane says. "You tryin to let every gusher in the forest know we're here? Jesus, Paul, you really are only good for one thing."

"Uh-uh. I'm good for a couple. Ask your mom," Paul retorts.

Lilly and I exchange a look. By the paling expression on her face, she can tell I mean to do something fast. I raise my gun and nod.

She shakes her head, motions to my sword. Even better.

I can kill them slowly.

14

"Here, horsey-horsey," the man named Paul says. He creeps through the copse of trees, his footfalls soundless across the forest floor. A practiced skill, one this man has learned in the apocalypse, no doubt. Lilly and I stay mannequin still, our bodies flattened against the rock as far as they'll go, which is not far.

Lilly makes a motion to me, saying she'll go left. I nod, and then I motion to the right. I'm going to sneak up behind them. Take them out before they even know what's coming.

Lilly's gun shakes in her hand.

"The damn thing is fuckin strung up," Paul says.

"Someone left it here," Duane replies. The

cocking of his gun follows his voice. "Be on the lookout. Could be back soon."

"Think this big guy's owners got eated by some gushers, I do." Paul is still approaching Bilbo with his knife out as my boots reach the asphalt. I'm quiet just like Paul. Traveling the wastelands has made me that way. The slightest sound—a cracking of a twig, too-fast breathing, the creaking of hinges—is enough to alert any nearby zombies, and they always seem to come at the absolute worst time.

"Don't think there's many gushers up here. Bandit keeps these woods clear. Matter of fact, this horse could be one of his," Duane is saying. He scans the woods as I take cover behind a nearby tree. I'm probably visible to anyone coming down the road from the farm, but right now I'm not worrying about that. Right now I'm worrying about not being heard. Once Duane thinks they're in the clear, he lowers his weapon.

"Doubt it. No sane person would just leave a horse in the forest. Like leaving an open box of pizza 'round a junkyard dog."

"I'm serious, Paul. Let's just get this shit over with. I don't like Bandit. He gives me the creeps."

Paul's voice is louder. I can't see him, but I'm

guessing he's not facing Bilbo anymore. "Damn it, Duane. You ruin all the fun."

"Hey, we unload this shit and find out it's not his, then we can come back and cook some horse. Sound good?" Duane is saying. He isn't the driver, but he's obviously the one in control of this dynamic duo.

"Soon as we mention a horse, that psycho is gonna come down here and cook it up hisself," Paul snaps.

"You don't know that."

"Let me just cut a piece off. I'll cook it up with the cigarette lighter. Small piece. They'll never know. Jesus, Duane, I'm so hungry," Paul says.

I decide this is the time to make my move.

Unfortunately, so does Lilly, except she hasn't developed the kind of stealth that I have. She is used to the loud bar, the unruly drunks, and the rowdy visits of passing-through District soldiers. So the rustling she makes by stepping too hard in a spot that shouldn't be stepped on is nearly nothing, but in the quiet of the forest and the situation, I hear it.

So does Paul.

So does Duane.

"Ambush!" Duane shouts.

Now Lilly's rushing steps are amplified. She even grunts as she lunges at Paul. I don't see her, but the struggle between them can probably be heard near the farm, which is not good. Not good at all. But what can we do about it? The concept of hope comes to mind. I won't let it linger. Hope is dead. Hope has been dead since 2016.

I step out on to the road, my sword in hand. I'm about fifteen feet from Duane so it's not a difficult throw. It's not hard to keep my blade from staying straight as it flies through the air and burrows into his right arm. The gun he holds tumbles to the ground, lost to the dead leaves and spotty grass. The muted black metal is swallowed by browns and dark greens.

He screams harsh and fast. I pounce on him, knees to his chest, breath whooshing from his lungs, cutting the scream off. I put my hand over his mouth for good measure, and what does this fucker do? He bites me. I grit my teeth with the pain and pull my hand away. He takes to screaming again.

And again, I cut him off. Two punches to the temple. Hard punches. And he's out like a light.

I notice a dab of blood on my palm from where he bit me. The wound doesn't look serious, just a chunk out of my index and middle fingers. It'll heal, and the guy's not a zombie, either. Thank God.

The urge to examine this new wound is great, to

sterilize and bandage it, too, but a voice makes that all but impossible.

"Get the fuck off Duane, you bastard," Paul says, except it doesn't sound exactly like Paul. It sounds like a man who's bitten his tongue and whose tongue has swelled up three times it size.

I look to the direction of the voice. Sure enough, it is Paul, and his nose is bleeding, red running around his mouth. He holds Lilly by the hair. I'm surprised because her hair isn't that long. He must have a piece of her scalp, too. There's a shallow cut below her right eye that's dribbling blood. Paul holds his own gun in my direction.

Fear tries to freeze me. Not because there is a gun currently pointed at my head, but because Lilly is in danger. Not because I care about her or Bilbo, but only because I don't want any more innocent blood on my conscience.

I'm not scared of the gun, either. I've been in this situation many times before. All I have to do is draw my own revolver and pull the trigger. Odds are that I'm a lot faster than this man on the draw. I'd bet my life on it. Will have to.

But I can't give what I'm going to do away, so I raise my hands and slowly rise off of the unconscious Duane.

"Stay there," Paul says.

My heart races. The smell of the kill is heavy in the air, like the smell and tang of electricity after a summer thunderstorm.

I'm already picturing how this is going to go down in my mind. I'm going to draw and fire in one smooth motion. Paul is going to die before he even knows what hit him. Then I'm going to kill Duane. But I won't shoot him. Better to not waste the ammo. No, I'll cut him up with the sword. Slice and fucking dice.

Lilly grunts. Something crunches. Paul lets out a high-pitched squeal.

Then he screams.

I'm too stunned to really comprehend what is going on. All I see is Lilly moving away from his grip and him falling over like a tree in a tornado. He drops his gun and holds his crotch.

Holy shit.

Lilly is on the gun, picks it up, and clobbers Paul's head with the butt of it. Blood spurts from the wound. His screaming ends, and for a long moment I think Lilly has swung hard enough to kill him. But as I examine his body, I notice his chest rises and falls raggedly.

Damn. Would've been better if she did kill him.

"What did you think I was going to do, sit around and wait for you to save me?" Lilly asks, walking through the stretch of forest to the road. "I ain't that kinda gal, Jack Jupiter. Not a damsel in distress. I can handle myself. Plus a gunshot would've given us away. I'd be fucking surprised if the screaming didn't."

I nod. About handling herself...I believe her. After that gruesome display, I'll never doubt her again.

She brushes past me with a slight smile on her face. Blood trickles down the swell of her right cheek. She spins something on her fingers. It catches the sunlight, glints like a disco ball. I turn away from it, but the jingling tells me that it's the keys to the U-Haul. I didn't even see her take them off of Paul.

"Let's find out what these dummies were hauling up to Bandit's farm," she says.

"You go ahead," I say, stepping over Duane. "After you tie that one up." I point to Paul. From my cloak, I pull out two lengths of rope, and tie Duane's hands to his feet. Lilly sighs with an expression that says *Do I really have to do that?* But she takes the rope reluctantly and does the job.

We'll need at least one of them.

So now I stand over Duane and raise my sword.

He's lucky to die by my sword. Lucky to not have to be torn apart by zombies or tortured by madmen like the one-eyed man or someone with the name Bandit.

"What are you doing?" Lilly asks, interrupting me.

"My job," I say.

"Leave him. For now. Could be useful," she says.

She's right. Damn. I lower the weapon and begin to tie him up. Then I drag him over to Paul and into the cover of the forest.

Lilly is back on the road, jimmying the key in the modified lock on the back of the U-Haul. I step into the forest towards Bilbo. The horse is spooked, but seems glad to see a familiar face, one that has no intention of eating him. His twitching slows and his eyes return to their normal sizes. I stroke his mane. "Sorry you had to be bait. Didn't mean for that to happen." I untie him and lead him out of the copse of trees.

As I do this, Lilly says, "Holy shit. Jack, you're not going to believe this."

My stomach drops. I'm trying to go through all the things that could possibly be in the back of the truck. Zombies? Corpses? Dead puppies? These guys seem like the type of people who might catch and kill puppies. I shake my head. No, that's ridiculous. What would Bandit want with dead puppies anyway? I'm just spooked, a little shaken from the near firefight. If one of us had shot off our weapon, every soldier on the farm would've known something was up. They'd be preparing for an ambush as we speak.

I round the corner of the truck and peer into the open space. What I see is like a gift from above. My jaw drops open. Lilly smacks me on the back.

Holy shit is right.

15

"Looks like they're planning to go to war," I say.

"This is the norm," Lilly answers.

On each side of the truck, there are racks and racks of guns—mostly assault rifles and shotguns, each one has either a tactical light or a ACOG scope attached to it. Heavy duty. In between the racks of guns are crates. A crowbar rests on top of one. I take it and pry it open. Inside the topmost crate is a bunch of straw. Inside the straw are grenades, about twenty of them. It makes me wonder what's in the rest of the crates. More grenades? A fucking *nuke*?

Lilly is tugging on my sleeve and this snaps me out of my surprise.

"Let's go," she says.

"Go?" I ask.

"We got what we wanted and more," she says, looking at me like I'm stupid. "A working car and an armory. We know where we're going, too."

I don't say anything for a long moment. I hadn't even realized this because I've been too distracted by our unconscious and tied up friends Paul and Duane. But Lilly is right.

"We move a few of these crates and Bilbo can fit in the back," Lilly says. "Not ideal but better than leaving him."

I still haven't said anything. I'm just kind of standing there with my thumb up my ass. Then Lilly is pushing me toward the front seat. "I'll drive," she says.

"What about them?" I ask, cocking a thumb toward the two tied up delivery drivers.

"Two choices and you know what they are," she says. "And I'm not killing them because they have a taste for horse meat. I got Paul there good enough. Felt his left nut shatter, I think."

My face screws up at her gruesome description. "Leave them," I agree. Their fate will probably be worse than the sweet relief of us killing them. I go back around the back and start moving the crates. They're heavy and the cords in my neck stand out as

I lift them. I'm happy to say I am still able to move them, though, just not as easily as I could've a decade ago. Father Time gets to all of us eventually. And sadly.

Lilly comes back from the forest, leading Bilbo by the reins. He goes easily enough into the back and fits almost perfectly, but if the ride gets rough, he might have a tough time. I'll make sure to go easy on the turns.

"I'll drive," I say to Lilly. "You get some rest. I'll wake you up in a couple hours."

She nods and though she won't say it, I can tell she's grateful.

I get into the driver's seat and start the truck. The engine hums beautifully, music to my ears. There's even a cassette tape in the middle console. It's Metallica's *Master of Puppets*. *Literal* music to my ears. I pop it in and keep the volume low.

For now.

Instead of backing up, I make a U-turn with the U-haul. Can't risk the beeping noise being heard at the farm despite it being about a half-mile up the road.

Something keeps nagging at my mind. I'm not the same man I used to be, but that man isn't completely gone yet, and that scares me.

He's in there somewhere, and right now he's screaming, telling me not to leave in the opposite direction of the farm, while the new Jack Jupiter, the tired, nihilistic Jack Jupiter who has lost everything is wondering what the fuck I'm doing. I can kick Lilly out, leave her with Bilbo. She'll be all right on her own. I've seen she can handle herself. I don't need the baggage weighing me down because this road ahead of me is not going to be easy; and if it ends in my death, I will be completely all right with that. That doesn't mean Lilly and Bilbo have to die because of me, though. It may come off as rude, she'll probably call me an asshole and say she hates my guts, but it's better than her being dead because of my recklessness.

I stop the truck, the brakes squeak.

"What are you doing?" Lilly asks.

I shake my head and hit the steering wheel with my open hand. "Damn it," I say because a different Jack Jupiter brings up the image of the poor people who were dragging the tractor, being chased by a group of zombies. No human being deserves such a fate.

But which Jack is going to win out?

Suddenly, a light pops on in my head. A compromise comes to me. I can save the people and get the other car. That way Lilly and I can safely part ways. Traveling by car is much safer than by horse. But will she go for that?

I guess I'll have to find out.

"What?" Lilly's eyes are as big as two moons. "Go, man!" she says.

"I can't." I cut the wheel again and turn toward the direction of the farm.

"Jack," Lilly says. "We don't have to go there."

I think of Darlene, of Junior, of Norm, of Abby. The man I was when they were with me, when our family was strong and together, would not let such injustices go unpunished.

"Yes, we do," I say. "What they're doing to those people isn't right. You saw what I saw. Imagine what they're doing to the others that we *couldn't* see."

"You're going to risk everything for some unknown people?" Lilly asks, her face a mask of utter disbelief.

Yes, I think, *and then we'll each have our own working vehicles and we can go our separate ways. I know we have common interests, but I can't stomach more innocent blood on my hands. What would Darlene think if she knew I was going to let those people suffer, if she knew I planned on ditching Lilly and Bilbo in the middle of District country? She'd tell me I'm a dumbass and probably slap me, which is less than I deserve.*

"Yeah, I guess I am," I say.

Lilly shakes her head—she's quite good at that. I'm expecting her to argue with me, to tell me I'm absolutely crazy. It's not my fault. I know if I let whatever's going on at that farm continue, I'll never get the images of a group of malnourished and miserable human beings running from a group of zombies out of my head. She doesn't argue, but sighs tiredly instead. "All right," she says. "It's your call. I trust your judgment."

And that's like a slap in the face. No one should trust my judgment. I don't even trust it, but I'm thinking of Darlene and Junior and all those that suffered at Haven and I just can't move on in good conscious.

Lilly pulls her gun out of her waistband, unloads the clip to check how many rounds she has left. "Well, what's the plan?"

A smile appears on my face. Is it a smile to cover up the fear that has taken up residence inside of me? Maybe. Possibly. Probably.

I can't say for sure. All I know is that this might be one of the stupidest decisions I've made in a long time. There's a large possibility of death or pain. But I don't care.

I have to look at the bright side. Even if I fail, at least I'll get to take down a few of those District bastards in the process. That's worth something, isn't it?

16

"The plan," I say, "is pretty simple. But that doesn't mean it'll be easy."

Lilly arches an eyebrow.

"I know." I'm nodding. "A bit cryptic. Here's what we're going to do."

Apparently my mind is made up. No going back now because I already have a plan. Man, what the fuck is happening to me?

Lilly leans forward to listen more intently. This makes me nervous, like I'm a college professor giving a lecture to a bunch of eager students.

I get out of the truck and open the back again. There's Bilbo. He looks glad to see me, glad to be free of the darkness. I lead him out. "Yeah, buddy, you're free for now." He whinnies in reply. Can't let myself get attached. I think of Cupcake, think of how much it hurt me to hold him while he withered away to nothing but skin and bones and matted fur. Can't experience that again.

I go through the weapons, taking one of the assault rifles off the rack. It has a scope on it. I aim down the road. It doesn't zoom much, but it'll be adequate enough. Lilly is out now. She watches me.

"Here," I say, handing it to Lilly. She tests the sight.

"Nice," she says.

"I'll drive the truck up to the farm under the pretense of delivery—"

"Bad idea," Lilly says.

I shrug. Yeah, it is, but what else do we have—

Unless...

We both look over to the clearing in the trees where Duane and Paul are tied, still unconscious.

"Take one of them," Lilly says.

"You read my mind," I say.

"Great minds think alike, right?" She nudges me with her elbow.

I nod, businesslike. No need to get jokey with her. Not when I intend to part ways once we get the car.

"If they're expecting them, they'll be a better

chance that they aren't suspicious of an unknown tagging along," Lilly says. She looks through the ACOG again. "So where does that leave me?"

"You ever shot long distance?"

"Not really," she answers. Uncertainty passes over her features, but it's so minor that I hardly notice because she's almost instantly back to her cocky self. "Doesn't mean I can't do it."

"But can you do it from horseback?"

"I can do anything, Jack," she says. "I've survived in this wasteland, haven't I?"

"Yeah, so have *they*," I say, nodding my head in the farm's direction. "That's why we can't underestimate them."

"Don't worry, Jack," she says. "We got this."

Her confidence surprises me still. I've never met someone so fearless, which is stupid. Can't be fearless in this world.

"You don't have to do this, you know," I say.

Lilly laughs. "You put this weapon in my hand, Jack. There's no getting rid of me now." She walks toward the trees, where Paul and Duane are. "Looks like our friends are coming back to reality," she says.

I follow her, bringing Bilbo with me. The wind blows and my skin prickles.

I approach Paul and Duane. Paul is the most alert, blinking almost comically while Duane stirs with his eyes closed, shaking his head back and forth. The wound in his arm isn't deep. Hardly any blood trickles out of it, but if he wants to keep living, he'll have to make sure it doesn't get infected. In a world where infection is rampant, that might be hard.

I bend down and look Paul straight in the eyes. He flinches at my gaze, and that satisfies me.

"Hey there, pal," I say.

He turns away from my gaze now, shocked over his current predicament.

"You District?" I ask, and the answer lies in the man's eyes. He looks at me with burning intensity, then, worried that he's given it away, he looks elsewhere.

"Nah, I ain't District. Neither is my buddy here. So let us go. He's bleeding pretty bad and my nuts have swollen up so big I don't think I'll be able to sit down for a solid month."

"That's if you make it another month, dirtbag," Lilly says, her upper lip curling and baring teeth.

I put a hand on her arm and give her a look that says *Calm down*. She nods halfheartedly.

"If you're not District, Paul, what the heck are

you doing driving a U-Haul full of assault rifles and grenades up to a District farm?" I ask.

He still won't look at me. He keeps looking at Duane, at the bit of blood dribbling out of the small slit in his shoulder. Now that I'm closer, I see I barely broke skin. The bastard hasn't lost nearly as much blood as he deserves.

"I—we wasn't. We was just on our way east," Paul says.

Duane stirs enough to open his eyes. He looks drugged and dazed. I must've really thrown him for a loop. Didn't even know I could punch that hard. I'll admit, that makes me feel kind of good. *Manly.*

"*What the fuck?*" Duane says, slurring, mouth thick with saliva and blood.

"Compromised," Paul says, and I'm surprised he knows such a big word. "Got jumped."

"Ah, my fucking shoulder." Duane turns his head to look at the cause of his pain and his eyes balloon three times their size. Any lethargy is blown away by this sight. "Did you stab me? What the fuck? Why do you have a sword like that? You the fucking Apocalypse Knight?"

I chuckle. I like the sound of that one.

"No," I say. "I'm just a regular guy who doesn't

like the assholes who think of themselves as people in the District."

Duane spits at me. He doesn't have enough energy for the bloody loogie to hit my feet—it lands about half a foot away from my boot—but nonetheless, it surprises me. "Well, we don't like fucking assholes with swords."

"That how you're gonna talk to the people who bested you, who *stabbed* you?" Lilly says. I put my hand up again. She ignores it, narrows her eyes and steps closer to Duane and Paul. "Show us some respect."

Duane surprises me once more. He spits again, this time getting more power under it. It *thwaps* against Lilly's thigh. She looks down disbelievingly, narrowed eyes unsure of what they've seen, and then she lunges at him with her fist raised.

I grab her around the waist to hold her back. She bucks and kicks and yells profanities I've never even heard, things I think she's made up but still sound just as dirty and insulting as the big C-word.

Duane has a bloody smile on his face, but Paul is uneasy. He doesn't like where this is going; he's scared. I don't blame him—Lilly is scary right now.

"Lilly, cool it," I say as calm as I can, but trying to hold her back has left me out of breath. "They'll get theirs. It may not be from you or from me, but they'll get it. Trust me. The assholes always do."

"No. They don't," Lilly argues. Her face is red. There's a sheen of sweat on her forehead. The longer bangs of her short hair stick to her skin. "So sometimes we have to give it to them. We have to give them what they deserve."

She has changed drastically from when she was telling me to leave them. It's funny what a guy spitting on you can do to your psyche.

"Yeah, which was exactly what I was going to do earlier, but you told me not to," I say. "I thought we were going to do this a certain way—"

She shakes her head. All the anger on her face melts. "You're right, gotta be better than them," she whispers and tells herself to take a deep breath. She does. Then she takes another one, and another.

"The bitch don't seem like she like me very much," Duane says from behind.

"You're going to regret messing with me," Lilly says, but then she's taking another deep breath. It's almost comical, their exchange.

"And you two are gonna regret fuckin with the District. They do terrible things to bitches like you. Things *I* don't even wanna talk about," Duane says.

Lilly stays calm on the surface. Underneath... well, I think that's another story.

"So you are District," I say. Not a question. As if I didn't know. I'm not surprised, the only bastards around left seem to be District.

"Damn it, Duane!" Paul hisses. "You just don't know when to keep your big mouth shut, do ya?"

"Oh, c'mon, Pauly, these motherfuckers ain't stupid. They saw what we're carrying. They know whose farm that is up there," Duane argues.

All Paul does in return is shake his head.

"Here's the deal," I say, taking my gun out of its holster. Both of the men get this look in their eyes, this look of fear that I like. I hate to admit that, but when you're the one in control of a situation like this, it feels good. "We're gonna do this delivery for you."

"Good luck, buddy," Duane says. He tries to shrug in his ropes. The movement is not very successful. "Bandit and the boys are expecting us. Me and Paul."

"That's fine. Paul will be there," I say. Seeing Paul's face twist up in confusion makes me happy.

"I will?" he asks.

"Sure. And I'll be right next to you, holding a gun

on your ribs, just out of sight of any District soldiers."

"What about me?" Duane asks. "You just gonna leave me here all tied up like a fucking hog."

There's a moment of silence as Lilly and I exchange looks. She shrugs. I shrug.

"Yeah, I guess we are," I answer. "Can't have your wound and swollen face give us away."

Duane's dark skin goes a few shades paler. "You wouldn't. I'll scream and they'll hear me up there."

"So will the zombies," Lilly says. "Who do you think is gonna get here first, the District preoccupied with a shipment of weapons or a horde of hungry zombies?"

"The lady has got a point," I say. "We saw a pretty big horde not too long ago. They looked especially ravenous."

Duane shakes his head, doesn't say anything. I walk over to Paul and cut his binds. "All right, Pauly old pal, you ready to get this show on the road?"

His legs are shaky and there's a deep fear in his eyes, but he nods. I hold my revolver to his back and force him into the car. Lilly comes around the side with me.

"Be careful," she says.

"I will. You too." Inside, I'm saying *Look at you,*

Jack, caring about people. But I know this would make Darlene happy. I can *feel* it.

She nods. "What's the signal?"

"If you get a clear shot on Bandit, take it, but if you don't, I guess the signal is whenever you start to hear gunfire," I answer. She smiles at that then turns to walk back into the forest. Duane is saying something I can't understand, spouting off obscenities, bloody spit flying. I think, for a moment, that Lilly is going to lay into him, shut him up. She doesn't. Instead, she takes a knife out. For the slightest of moments, I think she's about to kill him in front of God and everybody.

Nope.

She cuts the bloody rags around his knife wound and rolls them up into a little ball. Then she goes over to the ropes Paul was wearing and then back to Duane. She stuffs the cut shirt into his mouth and ties the rope tight around his head. Looks like he won't be screaming at all.

As I get into the truck, we catch eyes again. Hers are alive with adventure, with anticipation. She climbs up on Bilbo, the assault rifle slung over her shoulder, and nods at me. I nod back and shut the door.

"Start it up," I say to Paul.

"You guys are monsters," Paul says, never looking me in the eye. He does as he's told. The cab of the truck rumbles to life. Metallica plays softly over the speakers.

"We're all monsters," I reply.

17

We arrive at the farm's gates. Two men stand guard with weapons and grimaces on their faces. One of them sucks on a cigarette then exhales, gray smoke drifting up to the blue sky.

"One word about what's going on," I whisper, "and I pull the trigger."

Paul gulps and nods. "Making a mistake, friend. This ain't gonna end well for you or that girl."

"We'll see about that," I say. Maybe he is right. Now that we are here at the gate I'm left wondering why I'm doing this. Sure, I'm doing the right thing, I'm going to save these prisoners and take out one of the District's high ranking officers, but what if I fail? My mouth goes dry. I try to swallow but can't. My ultimate mission is revenge. Not against this Bandit guy or the other soldiers here, but against the one-eyed man. I know he's in Ohio. So what am I still doing here in Illinois?

Somewhere from the ether, I hear a voice. It sounds like Darlene's. I know that she is gone forever and what I'm hearing is nothing but an auditory hallucination brought on by fear and stress, but it's nice to hear her voice again so clearly. Even if it is my own imagination.

She says, *You're here, Jack, because you're a good person. You're one of the few good people left on this planet.*

But am I? In the two years on the road, I've done some bad things.

If I was by myself, if I was anywhere else, I would be crying. I nod to that phantom voice and think, *I miss you, Darlene. I miss you and Junior more than I can put it to words.*

We miss you, too.

Now Paul is rolling down the window, his arm working the crank. The guard with the cigarette jutting out of his mouth approaches. The cigarette rises nearly to his left eye with his smile. "Pauly!" he says. "How the fuck are you?"

"Good, Chip. Real good. Got a big order for you today," Paul replies. I no longer have the gun on him, but it's in hand under my cloak; there's also an assault rifle tucked between the side of the passenger's seat and the door, any visible parts obscured by my body. I'm sweating, my skin sticking to my shirt.

I wish I could hear Darlene's voice again. Not the hallucination, but the real one, the one that comes straight from her mouth because she isn't really dead. She's alive and we're back at Haven with Junior and Norm and Abby and Tim and Carmen and Eve, all growing old together.

The guard leans in closer, putting a hand on the edge of the window. "Who we got here?" he asks. "Where's Duane?"

An uncomfortable silence settles between us. There's tension, too. I hope I'm the only one aware of it. I think Paul is about to answer so I wait. He doesn't. I begin to open my mouth and just as I speak, Paul laughs and says, "This is Bruce. Didn't the boss tell you about Duane?"

Another bout of uncomfortable silence. This one doesn't last as long as the one before it. Chip rubs his chin and says, "No, I didn't hear about Duane. He all right?"

"Got bit," Paul says matter-of-factly. "Right on the

shoulder. Couldn't get him to the infirmary in time to amputate."

The guard takes his hat off and shakes his head. "That's too damn bad. That son of a bitch owed me coin. Worst Hold 'Em player I ever met." A gleam of reminiscence fills his eyes.

"I don't think he'll be paying ya back, Chip," Paul says. "He's gone. Put his own self outta his misery. It was bad. Real bad." Paul's lying ability throws me for a loop. This guy could be a hell of a storyteller.

"No sense in crying over spilled milk. What's done is done," Chip says. "He'll be missed, but we got work to do. Hear the Overlord is planning on expanding soon. Very soon."

"Heard that, too," Paul says.

This catches my ear more than anything else. Expanding? Nazi Germany and Hitler's plans for world domination come to mind, not for the first time.

"Heard they got a couple of jet planes up in the air on a test run," Chip says.

Paul nods. Judging by his lax expression he's heard this one. I haven't. Fear stirs my insides, my stomach roiling greasily. Jet planes? Fighter jets? Jesus Christ, where does it end?

"Oh well," Chip says. "Nice to meet you, Bruce."

He waves a hand and steps back from the truck. "You go on in. Unload in the garage. The boss'll be out in no time."

I raise a hand, subconsciously lowering my voice even though it doesn't matter. Chip and his buddy, along with the rest of the District here, will be dead before the sun sets. "You, too," I say.

The other guard pulls the fence open and Paul eases his way up the sloping gravel drive. It's about a quarter-mile long, probably a bitch to shovel in the winters.

"Jets?" I ask.

"I'm not answering nothing for you, you piece of shit," Paul says, not bothering to look at me.

I nod.

As we go up this drive, we pass the tractor. The zombies are still there, tethered to the front grill and tied to one another, but the humans are gone. I don't see any of them around at all. A barn stands near the left corner of the house. I'd bet anything that is where they keep their human prisoners, like livestock. To the left of the barn, parallel to the driveway are stables and the garage. There are two horses leaning out of those stables, big and well-fed. The roof is patched and the wood is old.

Now that I have a front view of the farmhouse, I

see just how nice it is, like one of those mansions so common in the South. It has a wraparound porch spotted with furniture. The paint job looks fresh and the outer walls are cleaned. The front yard is mowed in diagonal stripes all the way to the side of the half-plowed field we had seen from our forest vantage point. To our left and slightly behind us now is the windmill and a small pond with a rowboat in it. This brings back memories of the Mojave Desert and Central and Herb, but I push them out of my mind. Have to focus on the task at hand. There's no room for screwing up.

I wish I could ask Paul more questions, but he won't answer, especially now that we're inside the gates and he knows if I shot him, the entire brigade would be on me in a matter of seconds. I mentally list off the threats on the farm. So far I've seen the two guards at the gate with their weapons, a few men on the porch with rifles, and then the man who was once behind the tractor. Nowhere to be seen is the head honcho, the one Lilly calls Bandit.

What is it with the world ending and everyone taking on these lame monikers? I should call myself Jack Deadslayer just to fit in.

Paul turns off the driveway and onto a paved road branching around the various structures. He stops near the garage and the parked Lincoln and shuts the engine off.

"I hope you have a good plan," he says. His voice is chilling, quiet. "They are going to sniff it out as soon as they see you. You ain't District. It's written all over your face."

"Just like Chip back there sniffed me out?"

"They put him on the wall for a reason," Paul says. "Like the pawns in chess, man."

He has a good point. A sinking feeling in my stomach hits me. I try to ignore it.

Three guards are walking toward us. The garage opens with a sound of clanking machinery. I haven't heard a garage open in a long time, didn't know I missed it until now.

"Don't say anything you'll regret and you might live to see another day," I say to Paul. "Now get out."

He does and then so do I, putting my gun back in its holster. It wouldn't look too good if I got out holding my revolver with a white-knuckle grip, would it?

"Pauly!" one of the guards says with a smile on his face. The other two are already looking me over, confusion wrinkling their brows. These are the type of scared men I have seen following the District over the past two years, and it's that fear inside of them that makes them dangerous.

"Who's that?" one asks, pointing at me.

"Duane's replacement," I say coolly, but my right hand is ready to strike for my gun, while my left hand is itching to reach backward and pull my sword free. I don't have it. I left it in the back of the truck, it's just that old habits die hard.

As I'm rounding the hood, I notice out of the corner of my eye that Paul has stopped. He raises his hands, and this is where the sinking feeling present in my stomach bottoms out, and a spike of nausea hits me like a freight train. I almost double over with cramps, caused by fear, no doubt, but I can't because before the words leave Paul's lips, I have my hand on the butt of my revolver.

"He kidnapped me and killed Duane! Kill him! Kill him!" Paul screams, then he drops out of sight to the ground below, using the U-Haul as cover.

18

The first shot belongs to me, and I aim to kill. That's something Norm has tattooed on my brain. You don't waste your ammo, don't pull the trigger, unless you mean to blow someone's—or *something's*—head off.

So that's what I do. I don't feel guilty about it, not anymore. There was a time when I felt guilty about killing, a time when I hated the fact that I had to do it in order to survive. For as long as I was in Haven, behind the safety of those walls, I didn't kill another man. That was for nearly fourteen years. Then the one-eyed man came and did what he did and I was forced on to a collision course of rage and vengeance. I don't have any reservations as I pull the trigger. Especially when it comes to District soldiers. I told Lilly we have to be better than them, but that was a lie, a front. I was just trying to calm her down.

There's no point in staying on your high horse when survival is all that matters.

The first guard's face peels away and he drops to the ground, his head a bloody mess. The other one is not so slow. The smile he wore when he greeted Paul is gone, replaced by a savage grin of murderous intrigue. His assault rifle barks and sprays bullets at me. I dive back, taking cover behind the truck. Metal whines and the U-Haul bounces with the shots. To my right, I hear voices, thunderous footsteps. More guards are streaming out of the house, one, two, three.

One by one, I pick them off.

C'mon, Lilly, this is the sign! I'm thinking as more shots blast the grille of the truck. I have two shots left in my revolver before I have to reload.

Another guard bursts out of the front doors, nearly trips over the bodies of the already-fallen. I shoot him, one slug to the chest and he goes flying into the screen, taking it off one of its hinges so it now hangs crookedly.

The shots to my left have stopped.

For the moment, all is quiet except for the

groaning of the zombies, now enamored by all the noise, and the ringing in my ears. Then a shot hits much too close to my feet. A spraying of gravel nearly sends shrapnel into my arm. I spin around, see the guards who opened the gate running up the driveway, Chip in the lead.

One shot left.

Pressing my body up against the truck, I suck in a deep breath and close one eye. It's a long shot and pistols aren't known for being the most accurate weapon at a distance, but I don't have a choice.

My last bullet takes Chip in the stomach. He drops, dead. His buddy isn't too far behind him, though, and I need to reload.

What do I do?

"You're cornered, man!" the guard from around the front of the truck says. I hear shouting near the other side of the house, coming from the back where the field extends.

I back up.

"C'mon out and face your judgment," the guard says.

No fucking way, I think. I throw the passenger's side door open, dive in and grab the assault rifle I've stored in between the seats.

Just as I'm about to pop back up and shoot

through the bullet-starred windshield, the driver's side window erupts in a deadly rain of glass. My automatic instinct is to cover my face and eyes, but I quickly realize having to pick shards of glass out of my flesh is a lot better than being dead. As I move my hands, I see the long barrel and the shit-eating grin of the guard.

"Told ya, man," this guard says. "Now I gotta give you your judgment. Better me do it than the Bandit. He's a—"

But the guard doesn't get to finish. His throat bursts. An exploding fountain of red flies from a fresh hole below his right ear as thunder echoes behind me. I turn around, and through the passenger's side window is Lilly on Bilbo's back, the gun resting in the crook of her arm, the scope raised to her right eye.

Oh, thank God.

She waves a hand and then turns Bilbo around. They race along the fence, out of my view. I go out of the driver's side door, glass biting into my palms and forearms.

Another spray of shots behind me and I hope that it's Lilly taking out the other gatekeeper. No time to look. I need to beeline to the barn and set those people free. Easier said than done, of course. I take off and before I'm even three steps away from the truck, I hear someone say, "Hey, asshole!"

Shit, I forgot about Paul.

19

Paul is holding one of the assault rifles from the back of the truck. I hadn't even heard it open. I guess I wouldn't have with the shooting and all.

He opens his mouth to spout off his bad guy nonsense. Before he gets a word out, I shoot him in the gut.

He grunts, the words dead on his lips. The sandy color of his shirt, which is already stained with mud, now darkens with the color of his own blood.

"When will you assholes ever learn? Don't monologue. Don't even try to monologue," I say.

Sure, anticlimactic, but that's life. There'll be enough climaxes in the future.

He drops to his knees, still holding the wound, trying to keep his guts from falling out. It's a sad sight, really. I don't relish it or anything like that. Maybe Paul wasn't such a bad guy, maybe he could've turned had he been given a second chance. I don't know. But I do know he pulled a gun on me and I do know he was going to flay my horse and cook him for dinner.

I look at him as the life slowly goes out of his eyes.

Clopping of hooves. Lilly is coming up behind the truck on Bilbo. She sprays shots off toward the house. Over their echo she shouts, "Go, Jack! I'll cover you!"

I don't linger.

Running as fast as I can, I rush to the barn. There's a lock on the doors. I don't have time to think about anything besides breaking it.

I shoot at the padlock and it falls to the dirt, sending a cloud up around my boots.

The doors burst open, one of them hitting me harshly in the chest, almost as harshly as the smell hits my nose.

Zombies.

"Fuck," I say.

There's half a horde inside of the barn. I was wrong. I looked in the wrong—

"Help us!" a woman shouts. She's in the back of

the barn, her fingers gripping the bars of a cage. Inside are about a dozen people: men, women, children. They are dressed in dirty clothes, ragged, barely hanging on to their emaciated bodies. What kind of world are we living in where they cage humans and not zombies?

I stumble back as a rotter lunges at me. Rather than waste any of my ammunition, I club it over the head with the butt of the gun. The blow makes a sound like two bowling balls colliding, but it's not enough to kill it. It just falls backwards and bounces off the shambling bodies of the other zombies. There are about thirty of them. Not all of them have noticed I've involuntarily given them their freedom, and those who haven't are too distracted by the fresh meat they can't get to in the cage.

I keep backing up as the zombies stream out of the barn. The only way I can reach the people is by going around the whole building. There has to be another entrance to the human's side, a back door, otherwise there's no way they can get those people in and out without moving all thirty or so of the zombies at once.

Fear tastes terrible in my throat, almost as bad as the dead stink. Another lunges at me, two stick-like arms with loose flesh dangling from the bones swiping at my torso. I jump back. This zombie isn't even close. As it stumbles forward, I swing downward as if my rifle was a sledgehammer, and this time I get enough power in the swing to bust the creature's head wide open. Inky-black blood spills from the wound and the zombie twitches. The others don't care. They're unabashed by my feat of strength; all they care about is tearing me apart, chewing on my flesh. I break away from the pack as more gunfire erupts behind.

Only a select few keep their glowing eyes on me and fewer follow. The sounds and wide open space in front of them is much too enticing.

I round the back of the barn. There's another door here. The paint on the handles is worn away, and a thick chain and padlock snakes its way around them. I aim and turn my head, pull the trigger. The sound is monumental, *thump-thump-thump* on my eardrums. Some blood may be trickling down the side of my face. Whatever, no time to worry about that.

Once the gun smoke clears, the handles reveal themselves to be obliterated. I push the chain out and yank the doors open. The people inside have tears in their eyes; they're scared. So am I. Damn it, I am.

I'm with you, Darlene says.

So am I, Dad.

It's Junior's voice now. It hurts to hear it, but it's so sweet.

I'm so proud of you, he says. *Don't give up.*

Fighting back tears, I say, "Stand back," and aim at the cell's lock mechanism.

A young man with dark hair and a swarthy complexion says, "Look out!" and before I can turn around and see what he's pointing at, cold fingers wrap around my neck. The clicking of a dislocated jaw opens near my ear, muted by the never-ending reverberations of the gunshots that got me into the back of the barn.

Guess one of the dead followed after all.

It falls on me. I'm not sure if it was once a male or a female, but I feel long, greasy hair slapping down the front of my chest. Chances are it was a female. The gun drops from my hand, clatters off the dirt floor of the barn. The sound is muted, but I couldn't hear it anyway with the groaning right next to my ear. The breath of this beast is putrid, and suddenly, I feel the rough texture of a saliva-less tongue touching the right side of my jaw. Fear freezes in my gut and I get the sensation you get when you're coming up your basement steps in the dead of night, when you're sure there's something at the bottom, some beast, some monster—maybe a zombie?—waiting for you to stumble just once so it can pounce on you and drag you deep into the darkness where no one can hear you scream. I get this sensation and more.

My knees buckle because the zombie has fallen on my back, putting all of its dead weight on my shoulders. You would think I could handle this, but nothing weighs more than dead weight. Nothing.

I begin to fall.

Inside of the cage, the people are clamoring, some of them are screaming, calling for help.

I have to do something. I can't let it all end here, now, on some farm run by the District with a guy named *Bandit* in charge. No, I'm better than that, better than *this*.

Fight, Jack! Darlene says in my head. *Fight, damn it!*

Reaching inside of me for that inner strength, I find it has retreated to the bottom of my soul, farther than it has been since Darlene and Junior were brutally murdered. My fingers brush this strength, the tingling of it running through the tips.

If I could just—

My hand reaches back. I imagine I am drawing

my sword, only now I have to ignore the clamping jaws of some unholy creature in the process. My fingers find the zombie's stringy hair. I pull with all my might. My intention is to flip it over my shoulder, but death and disease have not been kind to the zombie's scalp and as I yank, I *feel* more than I hear its scalp give way. My clenched hand is in front of my face, and knotted between my fingers are clumps of hair, mottled with dirt, with blood, with disease.

Cold lips brush against my neck. Then teeth.

Would it really be bad to die now? Would it really be bad to reunite with my family, with all those who I've lost?

Fight, Jack!

Fight, Daddy!

Real voices or not, they're right. I have to fight.

I lean my head away, but that can only go so far. I have to do something else and I have to do it fast, before this monster rips a chunk out of my neck and ends me for good.

20

I do.

With the beast still on my back, the proverbial monkey, I rush forward. Each step is a pain and I'm afraid I won't build up enough momentum to shake it.

But I do.

Nearly falling on my last step, I ram myself into the cage. The solid steel beams rock me in the face, and to an outsider watching me do this, I probably look like the biggest idiot who has ever set foot on the planet.

Doesn't matter.

The explosion of the zombie's skull is both satisfying and revolting. What feels like a cold, diseased egg cracks on top of my scalp. Thick liquid and pus rolls down the sides of my face, and the dead weight crushing my shoulders somehow gets heavier.

A couple of the people inside the cell squeal at what has just happened.

I roll over and shake what's left of the corpse off of my body. The adrenaline coursing through me is enough for my muscle memory to take over now. I spring up and shake the brains and gore off. Unsurprisingly, most of it is as black as tar and as disgusting as only the insides of an infected, reanimated corpse can be.

I don't even have the urge to vomit as I look over what's left of the zombie. There's a mission to complete. Each second I spend feeling bad for myself, or sick, is another second closer the bad guys get to becoming victorious.

I pick up the gun, shake it a few times. Thick globs of brain fall from it. Then turning to quickly scan the door, making sure there's no zombies coming in for another surprise attack, and seeing there isn't, I aim down the lock mechanism and squeeze the trigger. The door practically pops open as sparks fly and thick, acrid smoke fills the air.

The men, women, and children inside are hesitant, looking me up and down. I see in their eyes that they wonder if they can trust me. I understand this, especially considering how I look. But there's no time to ease them into an escape. It's now or never. A war is being fought outside. Zombies are running rampant. Guns are going off like fireworks on a Fourth of July night.

"Go!" I shout, my voice serrated and harsh. "Get out of here. Run as far as you can."

A woman steps through first. The others seem to gather around her. She looks to be in her fifties, long, matted brown hair with a touch of gray, harsh wrinkles around her eyes and mouth—a woman who has spent more time out in the sun than anyone should.

"We can fight," she says.

"No," I reply. "Get out of here. You're free." Anger comes up my throat like bile.

"Monster!" a boy says from behind an older man. Before I turn around, I notice the boy wears a dirty, blood-stained burlap sack.

The zombie he has pointed out doesn't get to break the threshold of the barn before I put a single shot between its eyes. It falls back, arms out, yellow eyes dimming to black, the sweet black void of death. Of peace.

"We are going to fight. There is no denying it,"

the woman says. "If you do not have weapons for us, we will take pitchforks and rakes."

My mouth is a grim line. I'm resisting the urge to bite my lips into shreds. There is no convincing this woman.

Listen to her, Jack, Darlene's voice says. *She knows what she's doing.*

And now I'm really starting to question my sanity. For real this time.

"Fine," I say. "Those who can fight, fight, but someone has to lead the children to safety."

The man next to the boy in the burlap sack steps forward. As he does, I see his arm is not around the boy because that arm is not there at all. It is missing at the shoulder, a puckered red wound with jagged scars.

"I will."

I nod at him, hoping he sees the admiration in my eyes. Turning back to the woman, I say, "If you can get to that U-Haul, there's an entire armory inside." I'm pointing out the other door where the zombies have come from. The front of the U-Haul is barely visible. More guards have come out from the house, relegated to the porch as the thirty or so zombies push forward. I don't see Lilly. I don't see Bilbo. This worries me more than I care to admit.

The woman nods and turns to the rest of the people. "Revenge," she says.

The others echo her in a soft voice I can barely hear over the intermittent sounds of gunfire.

Then, to the man, "Be safe, Bob, and godspeed."

He nods and touches the woman lightly on her forearm. "Children, with me," he says. The five children, ranging from probably eight to thirteen years old gather behind him.

They begin to stream out. I go through the door, raising a hand as I peek around the corner of the barn. "I'll cover you," I say.

Only a handful of zombies too stupid to find all the action mill about in the yard by the truck. The closest of these is a shirtless man with a bloated right side. He is looking toward the road. His jerky movements remind me of C-3PO from *Star Wars*. I suck in a harsh breath, aim, and pull the trigger. The gun recoils, but my aim is true—as it almost always is. A small explosion of red on the zombie's head lets me know I've hit my mark. He falls lifelessly to the ground in a bundle of gray skin and twisted bones.

"Go!" I yell.

The woman takes off. She moves surprisingly fast for someone of her age. Then again, this is a woman whose most recent years revolve around pulling a tractor that weighs a couple of tons in the beating sun. She's going to be tough, no doubt about it. Still, I can't shake the uneasy feeling in my stomach.

I think it's because Lilly and Bilbo are nowhere to be found. The farm is big, but it's mostly flat. I would be able to see them... Unless something bad has happened.

Here I go caring again. Not good.

I don't allow myself to harp on the thought. Mostly because a zombie has caught sight of the few men and women who've taken off for the U-Haul. I aim down and shoot. The first two drop dead, clean headshots, but the last one is off. I strike its neck. A fountain of blood pours from the wound. The zombies don't notice, don't care.

I aim again. Can't let them get too close. One of the men has already noticed it and has slowed down. Fear is doing its age-old trick on this man, freezing him up.

Just as I'm about to squeeze the trigger, a horse bursts into my field of vision. Lilly is still on his back. Bilbo slices through the scene like a bolt of lightning, barely visible. She clobbers the zombie's head with the butt of her gun and yanks on Bilbo's broken reins. He shudders to a stop, rears up on his hind legs. Lilly dismounts quick and slaps him on the rump, then takes cover behind the truck with the freedom fighters. She is breathing hard, but somehow finds the strength to wave the men and women toward the spot where all the weapons are.

I spin around and check my left. It's all clear. Bilbo is running in my direction. The guards don't bother wasting their ammo on a riderless horse, and for that I'm grateful. He slows when he reaches me. I grab him by the reins and guide him behind the barn.

Now, scanning the horizon, I see the one-armed man with the children. He leads them to the far fence and the trees beyond. They are specks. I just hope no zombies coming from those dense woods spot them while they are there.

"Bilbo," I say, my voice loud. The horse's eyes roll crazily with fear. "Run toward them! Run toward them and help them to safety!" It's my turn to smack him on the backside. He takes off in the direction of the man and children. Will he make it? I don't know, and I don't have time to watch. I have to get Lilly and the others out of this war zone.

Spinning back around to face the truck, a barrage of gunshots rock it back and forth on its shocks.

thwap-thwap-thwap
creak-creak-creak

The last woman coming out of the back of the truck, clutching a rifle to her chest, is cut down by some of those bullets. She falls face-first, her lower body half-hidden behind the wrong side of the U-Haul. She twitches as the bullets hit her. One of the men yells out, "Claud!" and springs forward to try to grab her, but the older woman in the lead grabs his collar before he can do anything stupid. It hurts my heart to see the pain on his face, to see the tears streaming down his cheeks. I know all too well what it's like to lose your loved ones.

But I shake it off. Have to.

Lilly sees me and points above her head. I follow her finger. She is pointing to the roof. Two men holding long rifles have taken up residence behind the house's thick chimney. They pop out from behind their cover and blast off a few shots in revolving turns.

I wait for one, pull the trigger. It's not a headshot, but it takes him in the chest. He drops his gun; it goes sliding down the shingles, twitching the closer it gets to landing on the grass below, and then the man quickly follows after it. Like he's diving for dear life.

He lands no less than three seconds after his rifle does. It's about a three-story drop, and he's missed the grass altogether, hitting the concrete walkway to the front porch instead. The sound his head makes as it cracks against the hard surface is satisfying. And a little gross.

I'm waiting for the other guard to pop out.

He doesn't. Not after his partner has been cut down by me.

Still, the others on the opposite side of the truck are blasting at it, turning the metal into Swiss cheese. They seem to have an unlimited supply of ammo in the house.

Since the man on the roof is no longer shooting, I see this is my chance to regroup with Lilly.

Running as fast as I have in a long time, I get there just before the man on the roof musters up the courage to shoot. A barrage of bullets chase after me, spraying chunks of grass and clumps of dirt in my wake.

"Thought you were gonna cower over there all day," Lilly says. I can't tell if she's joking.

"Hardly," I reply. "We gotta take those people on the porch before they decide it's a good idea to surround us."

"We're pinned down," the older woman says.

The others—three men and two women of varying states of malnutrition and sickness—aren't talking, just looking back and forth to one and another in utter terror.

I nod at her. Yeah, we're pinned down, but this isn't anything new to me. I've been pinned down before, had my back against the wall, no way out, all that bullshit, and somehow always managed to get myself out of it. Right now is no different.

"Grenades," I say. "There's a box of grenades in the truck."

Before Lilly can ask what the hell I'm going to do with the grenades—*Blow us all to hell?*—I turn toward the back of the truck and I take off, hoping for Darlene or Junior's voice to help get me through this. *Needing* their voices.

21

SHOTS FOLLOW ME THE ENTIRE THREE STEPS IT TAKES to slip into the back. I have to avoid the corpse of the woman named Claud. Even in my haste, I note the lifeless expression in her eyes, the long rivulet of blood that flows from her nostril and the corner of her mouth.

Death.

All around us.

The *zing* accompanied by the heat of one of the shots in my direction almost throws me off balance. A step to the right and I'd be sporting a fresh bullet hole in my throat, lying right next to Claud.

Inside the back, I army crawl toward the stacked crates. Shots riddle the metal, dinging. Each one is just inches away from me. Dying sunlight streams through the holes. I slide one of the racks the assault rifles hang on between me and them. The rack thunders against my side whenever a stray bullet catches it. The pain in my ribs causes me to suck in sharp breaths through my gritted teeth, but it beats the hell out of getting shot.

Once I reach the crates, I wait for a lull in the gunfire before I even attempt to grab a handful of grenades. I mean, it has to stop sometime, right? They have to reload. No endless clips in this wasteland.

Sure enough, the moment comes. I strike the open box fast. Splinters dig into my flesh, but it beats the hell out of *bullets* digging into me. I grab a grenade then dive back to the metal floor, landing with a bone-jolting crash. On my way out, I don't take my time. I'm practically sprinting on my hands and knees—if that's at all possible.

As soon as I fall out of the back, I hear a snippet of conversation over the gunfire from one of the men, "—never make it," he says.

I drop to the grass and slide around the side, squatting next to them by the U-Haul's large tires. "Never make it?" I bring one of the grenades up to eye level and pull the pin. This isn't the first time I've handled grenades—there was a time in Washington

DC I had to pull the pin on one of these suckers to get out of a sticky situation.

They all look at me with sheer and complete terror, as if I just cut the wrong wire while disarming some sort of bomb.

I stand up, not afraid to get shot. The sudden urge to get rid of this thing in my hand is overwhelming. So I do.

For what seems like a long moment—but can't be any more than a second—the shooting stops. All is quiet on this farm, the zombies are not even snarling or dragging their dead limbs behind them like the trains of wedding dresses.

Then—

An explosion that I've not heard in a long time. The truck rocks with the force of it. For a second, I think it's going to fall over. Men scream only to have their yells cut short by fire and rage. The heat of the blast singes me through my pant legs, at my exposed ankles near the space beneath the U-Haul.

Then—

All is quiet again except for the ringing in our ears. I am struck by the horror of what could've occurred had Doc Klein been successful and carried out Central's plan. On a much, much larger scale.

"Nice throw," Lilly is saying, her voice muted.

"Thanks."

The aftermath of the explosion comes after my reply. The weary and pained voices of Bandit's guards, the sounds of jaws working and teeth gnashing into flesh, the greedy slurps, lapping tongues.

"Okay," I say to the rest of the group, but they don't look like they're hearing me. They look lost in their own horror, the battle-shocked faces of soldiers. "Let's clean this place up."

I roll off the truck and am not surprised to see both Lilly and the leader of the freed people on my right and left.

Smoke hangs low over the front yard and the porch, which has caved in, one pillar completely blown away. It came down on two or three of the guards. All that is visible of them are their boots, like three Wicked Witches crushed beneath Dorothy's house in Munchkin Country. Other guards were ripped apart by the explosion. Here, is a man huddled in the fetal position, a large wooden stake sticking through his gut and out his back. There, is a younger man face-down on the charred walkway, his body ripped in half, the intestines and vital organs hanging below his ripped and burned shirt like blood-red hoses, his legs are elsewhere, by the low bushes beneath what's left of the porch, which are currently burning. Two zombies have a tug-of-war with these legs for a moment as Lilly, the woman, and I are dumbstruck with terror and disgust, then they decide to just dig in, each ripping away the flesh as easily as if the skin were made of wrapping paper.

Lilly has a hand over her mouth. I don't know if she is about to scream or vomit.

At the end of the walk is Paul's body. Four zombies are feasting on him. They have ripped a large cavernous hole in his midsection. One of these zombies is currently on fire, not giving a shit about it, not feeling any pain. The other zombies are soaked in his blood.

I didn't like Paul and had even killed him, but no man deserves this fate. I raise the rifle and let off four shots. Each one takes a zombie in the head. The burning one falls back and smolders in the grass after a moment.

Lilly jumps at the sounds of the shots.

Of course, there are other zombies feasting as well. It seems there are more than there was in the barn, like they've been drawn to the farm by the chaos and sounds of war.

The woman turns to me and says, "They'll be

more men inside. Bandit doesn't fight unless he has to."

"For a guy named Bandit, he sounds like a pussy," Lilly says.

The woman nods. "Of the worst sorts."

"I'm Lilly, by the way." She sticks her hand out to the woman. For a moment, the woman just stares at it as if she doesn't know what the hell Lilly is doing, like handshaking is some alien concept.

Finally, she takes the hand and shakes it. It's awkward. "I'm Suzanna. My friends used to call me Suze. Now, no one calls me anything. It seems I have almost forgotten my birth name."

"Jack," I say, then it's my turn to shake her hand. And yes, it's quite awkward, like holding a deboned fish. "I don't mean to sound like a dick—"

Lilly cuts me off. "Not an easy feat for you."

Real funny, Lilly, but I'm not in a joking mood. Haven't been for two years. I glare at her and continue. "*But* I think it's better if we get to know each other after we clear this place full of rotters and District guards."

Suzanna nods and turns forward to face the battlefield. The others, I see, are sheepishly sticking their heads out from around the truck, their own guns held high. I hope none of their fingers are on the triggers because the slightest thing seems like it'll make them jump. Getting a bullet in my ass is not at the top of my priority list at this moment. Or ever.

I don't lead the way so much as the other women are keeping pace with me. At the foot of the steps, in the burning bushes, a weak voice begs for death. "Kill me. Kill *meeee.*" His face is a bloody mess, teardrops of red run down his cheeks.

I give this man what he wants, pulling the trigger and ending his suffering. Better than what he deserves.

Lilly and Suzanna break off. Lilly takes out the shambling zombies with a few pops of her rifle, shots I hardly hear or notice anymore; while Suzanna and the others club those zombies who are feasting on the dead.

We regroup at the steps. I nod toward the house and direct Suzanna and the others to surround it. Suzanna nods, bloodlust in her eyes. She wants this man named Bandit to suffer. I don't blame her. After directing the men and women to their spots, she comes up behind me.

"I'm coming in," she says.

I shake my head. "It's not safe."

"Don't tell me what's safe and what isn't. This

man and his followers have tortured me—*us*—for longer than I know. I will see his blood spilt if it's the last thing I do." Once she stops talking, her breathing revs up in intensity, nostrils flaring, chest rising and falling rapidly. She means business. I can see this in her eyes just as well as I can see the bloodlust. Who am I to deny her of this? Something tells me she wouldn't listen regardless.

I step aside and sweep my hand out. "I'll be honored to follow you," I say as I reach into my cloak and pull out a fresh clip, ejecting the nearly empty one. I put this one in my pocket now. You never know when you'll need more bullets—just one can separate you from life and death. This is not a Norm-ism as you might think it is; this is something I've picked up on my own journeys, from my own experience.

She nods and heads up the steps. The porch creaks beneath our weight. For a moment, I think it's going to cave inward and the road will end here. We'll be buried beneath the hot rubble like the soldiers to my right. And would that be so bad? Certainly better than going out by way of zombie. It doesn't happen, though. We keep going.

Inside of the house, it is fairly normal once you get past the stars of glass on the rug and the few limbs that have made their way through these broken windows.

"Split up," I say, pointing Lilly to the left, Suzanna to the right, and me up the stairs.

As I take the bottom step, I hear Lilly scream. A gun goes off and my heart freezes in my chest upon hearing it. Luckily, nothing else freezes. I spin around and see a large, hulking man—who would put both my old friends Herb and Kevin (the professional bodybuilder) to shame—run over Lilly like a running back. She takes most of the hit on the shoulder. It spins her in a circle before she crashes to the carpet, glass crunching beneath her body. This angers me more than I care to admit. My own bloodlust burns in my eyes. I feel it smoldering. I raise my gun and let a burst of shots loose, but the man known as Bandit is too fast. He disappears through the doorway, not bothering to throw it open. Instead, he goes through the wood. Shards spray in all directions. A cloud of saw dust masks his escape.

Clamoring outside. Shouting, screaming, then... shooting. One shot goes off and then another. The screams replace it. I don't let the sound of battle hold me back. I rush toward the unhinged door and just as I'm about to go through, I hear something else, something I never thought I'd hear again.

A voice, but not just any voice.

"Bandit? You there, Bandit? FF4356, come in. I repeat, come in, FF4356." I would know this woman's voice even if I was deaf. I stop and turn to the sound. It is coming from the room Lilly had gone into, the room where Bandit had rushed from. Lilly is on the floor. Absentmindedly, I reach down and help her up. Her eyes burrow into me, but I hardly notice.

That voice.

"Abby?" I say.

But there's no way. She's been gone for two years. Is it like the way I've heard Darlene and Junior's voice? My own hallucination?

For a second, I think I've gone insane, *really* insane. A shot blasts through what's left of the front parlor window, causing Lilly to scream in surprise. I don't flinch, not even as I feel the rain of glass at my back.

That voice. That impossible voice.

"Jack, get down!" Lilly is saying.

Stray bullets are flying in all directions, thudding into the house's siding, eviscerating the wooden door even more than Bandit has. Suzanna has left us. I didn't see her go, but I no longer sense her presence.

"Jack!"

A hand clutches around my ankle. It's death-gripping my pants. I'm moving to the sound of that voice, pulling away from Lilly.

"Jack, what the hell are you doing?" Lilly yells. I am at the bottom of a pool, barely aware of her speaking to me at the surface.

"FF4356, what's your status? I repeat, *what is your status?*"

It's Abby's voice. It has to be. I would recognize that flair, that bite, in her tone anywhere.

Now I'm running, running away from the screams and the fresh sounds of gunfire outside. I cross the room. A grand piano to my left. A fireplace to my right. A doorway in front of me. Through this doorway I go.

No longer do I hear the voice; now, I hear a crackling—the feedback of a long-distance radio. It reminds me of walkie talkies, only amplified.

"FF4356, come in!"

There it is, the radio. It is a large gray box with angry red lights blinking on its face. Next to these lights are thick dials. Curly rubber wires hang from each side of it. Three longer wires hang from the back and plug into a power strip in the wall.

It takes everything I have to move my foot forward. Each step is conscious, deliberate. On top of the radio sits a headset. I pick it up, slide it over my messy head. The speakers don't work because the voice is played aloud, but the microphone does. It has to. Why else would it be plugged in?

"Abby?" I say, my voice barely a whisper.

No voice answers.

Maybe I am crazy.

A long moment passes. It feels like eternity to me, like the blurring days after Darlene and Junior were murdered.

"He's getting away!" one of the women with Suzanna yells outside, voice muffled.

I can't stand here and wait. I have to go out there and help. So turning around, ready to run back out to the battle and forget the phantom voice I heard—

"Jack?"

No, I think. *No, this is impossible.*

But it's not. That voice right there is Abby's voice, thick with pain and confusion.

"Abby?" I whisper. Then, gaining more power, "Abby!"

On the other end of this radio line comes more static. It's like someone is wrestling over the controls with her.

No. No way. It's really Abby, but someone is onto her. Just my luck. My head spins. Heart thumps my sternum. I feel sick, dizzy, all of the above.

"Jack, Chicago. We're in the Black Towers," Abby says, and I still can't believe what's going on. My stomach clenches with excitement and nausea and fear. I might throw up or I might run to the rooftops and scream at the top of my lungs.

"The Black Towers?" I ask, my voice getting stronger still. Living in Chicago for a few years before this all happened, I have never heard of the Black Towers.

"I don't have much time, Jack. Come to the Black Towers."

"Abby?"

No answer.

The line goes dead. I stand there for a moment clicking buttons and tweaking knobs. Feedback screams in my ears. My back prickles with sweat, my palms are slick.

"Abby? Please answer me. Let me know I'm not crazy," I'm saying, because that is what this feels like, some kind of crazy dream.

Again, there's no answer. I try to rationalize what has happened, what I heard, but I can't. Nor do I have the time to because the yelling outside hits me like a tidal wave. The gunshots, too.

"Jack?" Lilly says behind me. Her voice causes me to jump. If my finger had been on the trigger of my rifle, I would've sprayed a few bullets into the nice lacquer floors.

I turn around. I must look pretty fucked up, judging by the crooked way Lilly is looking at me.

"I—"

"The Black Towers," she says almost dreamily.

"You heard that?"

She ignores me. "Jack, Bandit's getting away. We need to help." Her eyes have gotten bigger; the dreamy quality to her voice is gone.

I nod. Time to worry about this later, I think, still not totally believing what has happened.

Pushing past Lilly, I go out the front door. There, lies one of the men I freed. He is no older than me, as skinny as a rail, as gaunt as a zombie. A fresh red hole is in his throat and his eyes are closed. The sight makes me sick and angry. I scan the front yard, looking for the man they call Bandit. Before I can locate him, the sound of a revving engine gives him away.

Shit. He's in the Lincoln and he's flooring it, tearing through the grass and the gravel and the zombie corpses. One tire bounces over a dead body —I can't tell if it's zombie or human—and it leaves a bright crimson streak on the driveway.

"Suzanna!" Lilly shouts.

The crazy woman has jumped in front of the careening vehicle, her rifle raised. She pumps off a few shots, but the car keeps coming. Sparks fly and glass cracks as the bullets register home.

Dread invades me as I see she has no intention to jump out of the way. For her, right now it's kill or be killed, and the odds are definitely leaning toward *be killed*.

I don't think about what I have to do. I just do it. That's how it works in this wasteland. If you hesitate, if you think too long or too hard, you make a mistake, and mistakes will now literally cost you an arm or a leg...or your life.

The rifle rests on my shoulder. I suck in a deep breath and hold it. No clean shot in the driver's side window, so I aim for the back tire.

The rifle barks twice.

Both shots hit the mark and the sound the rubber makes as it explodes seems to rival the sound the grenade made earlier.

Bandit is going fast, but he's not going fast enough for the car to flip out of control—thank God, because that's my ticket to the Black Towers. Instead, he fishtails, swerving out of the way of Suzanna, just missing her by a few feet.

Turns out, she jumps at the last possible millisecond.

"Nice shot!" Lilly says in my ear.

Not over yet, I'm thinking as I rush to the still moving car. He's jerking the wheel. Rubber shrieks and burns, clumps of grass and dirt fly. A cloud of gray smoke fills the air.

I stop in my tracks when I see where the Lincoln is heading—right for the small duck pond at the foot of the windmill.

No. Please no.

Spinning, the car comes to a rest right on the edge of it, sending whatever birds were floating there lazily up into the darkening sky. The front passenger's tire nearly touches the water.

Too close. My heart begins beating again and I rush to the scene.

Suzanna and the Hispanic man beat me there, just as Bandit opens the door to make a break for it. He has a chrome pistol in his hand, it catches the light and sends it back at us like its own form of deadly projectiles.

Before he raises it, Suzanna's gun goes off.

The sound of a gun is enough to make me stop in my tracks, almost always is. You wonder if you're getting shot at or if you've been shot...or if you're dead.

None of those things happen to me.

The first bullet takes Bandit in the chest. He's a big guy, so he barely jerks with the movement. Then the next shot—whether it comes from Suzanna or her friend, I don't know—hits him in the stomach, sprays blood. He drops to his knees groaning.

I almost want to tell them to stop. I need to question this man, need to find out more about the one-eyed leader of the District and the Black Towers, but I see in their stony faces that they have no intention of stopping until Bandit has suffered as much as he has made them suffer.

He puts his blood-slick hands up in a last-ditch gesture of surrender. No luck. Suzanna and her cavalry have pulled their triggers one last time. The succession of shots rips Bandit's broad jaw line into pieces. He flies over the hood and lands in the duck pond with a splash, leaving a rain of blood on the Lincoln's paint job.

A long silence follows this. Something great has just happened between these men and women. They have solidified their freedom. All I can think about while they wrap each other up in teary-eyed hugs is Abby.

She has been with me since the beginning. Together, we have taken down warlords and scores of zombies. Once, just outside of DC, Abby was bitten. I carried her in my arms, this sister I never had, to a place of safety where a man named Jacob performed an immediate and gruesome amputation. I remember how I felt when I thought I lost her that time, how I thought the world was ending. But she came through. In only about a day's worth of time, she was almost back to her normal self. That's Abby for you, tough as nails. Then the District attacked Haven and I lost my wife and son and sister-in-law and so many others, including Abby, and I really did think the world had ended...for real this time. An apocalypse after the apocalypse.

I heard her on the radio, and so did Lilly. I'm not crazy, I'm not hallucinating. Abby is all right; she's alive, but why is she communicating to Bandit's farm via District frequencies? This is the question burning up inside me as Lilly breaks away to my right and helps Suzanna drag their dead friend out of the grass and up to the concrete.

I can't just stand here and not help.

I walk over there with them, help carry this bleeding man away.

Suzanna tells the man who had helped her take

down Bandit to give the signal. This confuses me for a moment before the man raises his rifle into the air and shoots. One shot...two, three, four.

"Let's hope they made out better than we did," the man says. He looks at me, sees my arched eyebrow.

"Bob and the young ones," the man says. He sticks his hand and we shake. His name is David. He introduces me to the other men and women. There is Marco, Daphne, and Malorie. Eric is the one who has been shot in the throat, resting eternally at our feet. When this somber moment ends, David says, "That was good shooting back there, taking out his tire like that."

I shrug. I don't need praised for doing the right thing. I only acted on instinct.

"Surprised you did," Lilly adds, "with how spaced-out you looked. Still kind of do." She looks at me warily. In this look, I can tell we have a secret. I'm grateful for her not bringing up the fact that I had a clipped conversation with someone over District airwaves. It would raise too many questions that I'm not prepared to answer. Lilly looks away and helps Suzanna off of her feet. With the battle over, with Bandit dead, this woman, who was a slave no less than an hour ago, looks exhausted and older than her actual age. The tan she wears from constantly being out in the sun pales. She's crying silent tears.

"Yes," Suzanna says. "Great shooting, Jack." She musters up a slight smile. "I would have got him anyway."

I chuckle. "I don't know about that…" My tone is joking, but I'm really not. If it wasn't for me, Suzanna would be roadkill.

"There they are," the other man says, shielding his eyes from the waning sun. On the horizon, Bilbo walks, specks on his back, specks next to him. It's the one-armed man and the children, back to the safety of this farm. Though how much longer this place will be safe, I have no idea. With the gunshots and the grenade explosion, it's bound to draw unwanted attention—zombies or others.

We can't worry about this yet.

I say, "If we start walking now, we'll meet up with them about halfway, I think."

"We aren't going anywhere, Jack," Suzanna says. "There is no safety out there."

"No safety in here. With all that noise we made, a horde is bound to be on their way," I argue. This shocking revelation is supposed to knock them off of their feet. It doesn't.

"Let them come," David says.

Daphne nods, fresh tears in her eyes. "We'll be ready for them."

"We have the weapons and we have the manpower. When they come, we will put them back in the ground where they belong," Suzanna continues. "This is a good place. The soil grows and the water flows."

"What about the District? They're bound to show up sooner or later," Lilly asks, honest fear in her voice.

"We'll be ready for them, too," Marco says. He is the youngest of the bunch, Hispanic, a man no more than twenty years old, fifteen of those years spent in an apocalyptic wasteland. I can't help but wonder if he remembers what it was like before all of *this* happened.

Now the freed people stand shoulder to shoulder. On their faces, you can see this bond, this camaraderie. They are a family; what I once had all those years ago. They have found their Haven and there's no taking it from them.

But I know what happens to family. It's ripped apart in this wasteland. The evil always wins out and the good always die. Like I've said, it's not easy to have a family when the dead walk and hunt us like animals.

There is no convincing them, though, and it's not my job to do that, either.

"Well," I say, "let's get rid of these bodies before the others show up. The youngins don't need any more scarring than they've already had."

I can see Lilly smiling out of the corner of my eye.

"Thank you, Jack," Suzanna says. She smiles, too. It is somber, melancholy. She sticks her hand out and I take it. She squeezes, grateful for my help. I pull my hand away. Can't get sucked into another trap, of caring for people that will only end up dying.

The clean up begins. Each one of us is tired and hungry and—at least I am—afraid, but we drag the bodies to the back of the house. The District guards and the zombies go in one pile, while the other freed people who have lost their lives go elsewhere. They mean to bury them, and I mean to help. If anything, it's a way to make up for the fact that I didn't get this chance in Haven, a way to atone for that sin.

Marco, David, and I go around with knives and stab each corpse in the head, killing the brain even if they've already been shot somewhere close by. Better safe than sorry, we're all thinking.

The rest start a large fire after this and the air fills

with the sickeningly sweet smell of charred flesh with an undercurrent of burnt hair.

Daphne disappears into the barn and reappears with two shovels. Lilly and I offer to dig the holes as they rest. Well, mostly *I* offered and Lilly reluctantly agreed.

The night has come now, but it doesn't seem like it with the large bonfire at our backs.

Bob and the children have made it here. The smell in the air is unmistakable, and they paid it no attention.

Bilbo roams free, comes over my way. I give him a reassuring nod he doesn't understand then prances off like he doesn't know me. Good, I think, let's keep our relationship like that.

"He's going to make some new friends," Lilly says, leaning on her shovel. I follow Bilbo with my eyes, and sure enough, Lilly is right. The horse stops by the stables and examines the other two horses, who are sticking their heads out of the dark. Their ears move back and forth, along with their eyes. Somehow, I think this is their way of communication.

A boy of maybe thirteen guides Bilbo into an empty stable.

Then we're back to digging graves for the freed people—our new friends.

It takes nearly another half-hour before the graves are dug. We took our time, or at least I have. When I got done digging my hole I began on the second, then Lilly came to help me out.

Suzanna and the rest come out of the house. They have washed up, put on better clothes. Some of the children wear oversized and baggy shirts and pants. Some of the women wear male sweatpants, tied over and over again at the waist to fit. Suzanna has scrubbed the dirt from her face, washed her hair. She looks stunning as only a woman of her age can. Matured beauty.

Marco and I carry the wrapped bodies to the edge of the graves. Others offer to help, but I refuse them.

The funeral is as beautiful as a funeral can be. Many tears are shed and hands held. Hugs and kisses and all the usual stuff. I watch with dry eyes. It's not that I'm not sad or not heartbroken for the lives lost today or anything like that, I'm just so used to death that I've become numb. The only thing that gets me these days is thinking of Darlene with her throat slit and my own son with a bullet in the back of his head, lying lifeless on the blood-soaked ground. I try not to think of these things. My brain doesn't always comply.

Plus, I know this won't be their last funeral. The funerals are constant in the wasteland.

We bury the bodies. Everyone helps with either shovel, spade, or their bare hands. These three dead men and women rest eternally by the small duck pond where the cause of all their pain and trouble lies at the bottom, half his face blown away courtesy of Suzanna.

After the dirt is packed and the crosses made from the ruined porch are planted, the crowd disperses.

Lilly and I don't move for a minute. Me, because my head is somewhere else, deep in thought over Abby's voice. I still can't believe it. Was it really her? Lilly doesn't move because of how troubled I am, I think.

I look at her, see a question on her lips.

"What is it?" I ask, beating her to the punch.

"Are you— Are you District, Jack?"

I snort with laughter, but there's hardly any humor in the sound. "Me, District? You gotta be kidding. Did you not see what I did? Did you forget about all the Districters I killed today?"

She weighs her words carefully before speaking

them. "I don't know...the District is crazy enough to do something like that."

I shake my head. "Ridiculous. I know you don't really believe that."

"Maybe I don't." Lilly leans closer. "But I'm confused, Jack. When Bandit escaped and knocked me down, I heard you talking on the radio. I heard the woman's voice on the other end replying to you as if...as if she knew you."

"She does."

Lilly squints. "Who is she? Why is she District?"

"I—"

Suzanna's voice cuts me off. We turn around to see her on the slanted steps, waving us closer. "Jack! Lilly! Come inside."

I take this opportunity to put Lilly's question on the back burner. I walk to the house, the Black Towers and Abby on my mind.

The truth is, I don't know why Abby is in the District or how she's even alive. After two years of not hearing her voice, of believing her to be dead, I'm still not sure if it was real, even if Lilly heard it, too.

22

The inside of the house has been hastily cleaned up. A wonderful smell drifts down the hallway. It's the smell of cooking food.

Suzanna puts a hand on my shoulder, guides me inside. I have to duck so I don't bang my head on the caved-in porch roof.

"You aren't trying to leave us, are you?" David asks.

Lilly speaks over me. "No, why?"

"We're having a feast. Broke into Bandit's storeroom. There's more food in there than a damn Walmart," David answers.

"Come on," Suzanna says.

She leads us to a large dining room. A table stretching the entire length of the house, I swear, sits in the middle. The carpet is a burnt orange and the wallpaper looks freshly and professionally hung. The others sit at this table.

Lilly and I take seats near the end, next to the one-armed man.

"Thank you," he says to me, crying.

I shake my head. "It's nothing. Don't thank me." And I'm not trying to sound like some cocky asshole who knows it was definitely something. Nothing like that.

"Yes, it is. It's more than you know," Bob, the one-armed man, says.

A little boy looks up at me with big eyes and says, "Thanks, mister." The other children join in as the adults smile at them, proud of their manners. These are kids who have known nothing but the apocalypse. They've grown up in a world where there are no manners yet they somehow have them.

I smile back. "Really, it's—"

Lilly hits me on the shoulder, like Abby would've, and says, "Just take the compliment, Jack."

I nod. "It's what my wife would've done," I whisper.

"Is she your wife, mister?" the same boy asks.

Lilly and I chuckle awkwardly, but a throb of pain seizes my heart, a throb of pain for Darlene.

"No," Lilly says, then leans over to a teenaged girl and whispers all-too-loudly, "but he wishes."

The girl giggles.

"What happened to your wife?" the boy asks.

"Now, Tommy, leave Mister Jack alone," Bob says.

Tommy mutters an apology. By this time, the first rounds of food start arriving on the table, brought in by Suzanna, Marco, Malorie, and Daphne. There's a pan of steaming bread, a dish of cheesy macaroni, canned vegetables with a spoon in them—green beans, corn, tomatoes. Powdered milk and glasses, water with ice cubes, and even a few dusty cans of Coca-Cola. It's not much when you look at it, but as you bring the first forkful of macaroni up to your mouth and take a bite, you realize it's everything you've ever wanted and more.

We eat and laugh and get to know each other.

The one armed man's name is Robert, but he prefers Bob because, he says, "It makes me feel younger than I am." He lost his arm in Iraq, long before the zombies came. He's been living with this particular handicap for a good amount of time and now he hardly notices it, though he'll more often than not feel that phantom arm like it's still there. "Itches like crazy. That's something, huh? An arm that isn't there, itching."

Suzanna was a librarian many years ago. She stayed in her branch for nearly six months after the government decided to tell us all to fuck off. They were doing a local food drive and the break room had a microwave and a good amount of bottled water. A backup generator, too. She survived more or less by herself, reading every book in the library once in that span of time. It was all she could do, she said, to take my mind away from the horrors happening all around us.

"Did you ever read *The Deadslayer?*" I ask.

She looks to be deep in thought. After a moment she nods. "Wasn't a favorite of mine, but as far as zombie books go, it was fun." She looks at me crookedly, a slight smile on her face. In those eyes, I can tell she knows. "Why?"

"Because I wrote it, along with a handful of other B-grade horror books," I answer.

"Jack Jupiter," she says softly. "I thought I knew that name."

"Funny how things turn out, huh?" I say.

She laughs and like most laughs you hear nowadays, the sound is humorless.

Lilly tells her own sad stories. How she was taken from her hometown when it first started by the military, how their base was attacked, completely obliterated. She escaped. She doesn't mention her pregnancy, and I'm glad. I don't think I can handle listening to that story again. Besides, the youngins look to be deep inside of their own minds, but I remember being that age, remember playing grownups for fools, listening when I probably shouldn't have been. I think Lilly senses this, too. Then again, these kids probably have their own messed up stories. I was a kid when the world had order. Things are different now. Much different.

After these stories are shared, a silence falls over the group. It's a comfortable silence, the silence of friends who don't need to fill the void with unnecessary conversation. And after all that has happened today, many of us probably don't feel like talking much more.

We eat a dessert of green Jell-O. It doesn't taste as sweet as I remember, but it hits the spot nonetheless. Everyone's lips, teeth, and tongues turn green. The kids get a pretty big kick out of this. Seeing them laugh and point at each other breaks my heart. I think of Junior, I think of how he'd act and this thought stabs my heart with icicles of sadness. I'll never be over losing them.

Lilly puts a hand on my forearm. It startles me

out of my thoughts. "Jack, you look exhausted," she says.

I nod. I am.

"Why don't you get to bed?" Lilly asks.

The idea of sleeping here hasn't really occurred to me. I know if I stay to long, I'll get attached. Can't let that happen.

Looming in the back of my mind are the Black Towers, and Abby trapped at the top of one of them, waiting for me to come rescue her. Still, much needs to be done before I can travel to Chicago. I have to change the tire on the Lincoln, have to load up on ammo, have to figure out a way to let Lilly know I'm leaving her behind on this farm with these nice people at a place where I believe she'll be safe, where Bilbo can roam and eat and be taken care of without running, because a life on the run is no life at all.

Suzanna gets up, her chair's legs brushing against the carpet. The rest follow suit. I begin to gather up the dishes and the crumpled napkins. Bob tells me to quit it, to go get some rest. "Don't worry about the mess. We'll handle it."

"I don't mind," I say. "It's the least I can do after you all cooked for me."

Bob looks at me with serious intensity. It almost

makes me shift my eyes elsewhere. "Mr. Jupiter," he says and as he speaks he grabs my hand. His own hand is arthritic and gnarled and covered with rough calluses, looking much older than this man actually is. He squeezes. "I didn't expect to sleep anywhere with a roof over my head that doesn't leak. I didn't expect to have covers or food besides old bread and rusty water. Look at me now—look at *all* of us. We're sitting here like kings and queens, all because of you and your bravery."

I nod, resisting the urge to say it wasn't a big deal. Lilly grabs my other hand and says, "C'mon, hero. We need to talk."

We leave the smiling faces of the freed people and go out to the living room. Once we're out here, I can't help but keep looking at the radio. Part of me wishes Abby would call my name again while the other part of me plainly sees that the radio has been unplugged and pushed up against the wall. No voices will be coming from that box, that's for sure.

Lilly notices my eyes jumping back and forth from her to the small room. She snaps her fingers in front of my face, says, "Jack? Hello?"

"Sorry," I say.

"Okay," she says, grabbing my arm and dragging me out of the house. The door bangs behind us. The air is thick with the smell of smoke and burnt meat, but it's a nice night: clear skies, bright moon, light breeze. I scan the horizon for the inevitable horde of zombies. There isn't one.

Maybe, I'm thinking to myself, things are starting to go my way for once. I mean, it's been two years without much luck. Is it too much to ask for a little? I'm overdue.

"You're not leaving me behind," Lilly says, again her voice snapping me back to the here and now. This is not what I expected her to say. "I'm not stupid, Jack. I know that's what you intend to do."

Her clairvoyance is a bit alarming. Is it that obvious?

I try to find the words to reply but can't. I stand in front of Lilly and for the first time in a long time, I notice that my shoulders slump. Posture is everything, that's what Norm always said. You stand up straight and you project this confidence about yourself. Right now, I pretty much project no confidence whatsoever, and I should, shouldn't I? I just helped free a bunch of human lives, I helped take down a bunch of District scum, I've discovered that a long lost family member is still out there. So why do I feel so...bad?

It's not that you only feel bad, Jack, my mind says,

it's that you're also scared. Scared shitless. Abby is alive, she's out there, but she's in District territory. That means Norm can still be alive, too. What makes you feel bad is that you know Darlene and Junior and Carmen and Tim aren't out there. They're dead and gone and this is somehow a brutal reminder of that. Talk about pessimism.

Lilly snaps her fingers again. "Okay, next time you space out on me, Jack, I'm not snapping my fingers. I'm gonna smack you across the face instead."

I nod. "Probably deserve it."

We talk in hushed whispers. It's a natural reaction to life on the road, staying quiet so zombies don't hear you…all of that jazz. Really, staying quiet is the least of my worries.

"Oh, shut up," Lilly says. She tilts her head back and takes a long, exasperated sigh. "Snap out of this funk and tell me what is going on."

I inhale deeply. "Okay," I say.

23

After I tell her why I don't want her coming along, after I practically beg her to stay here, Lilly's voice grows cold and much, much louder. "You're not leaving me behind. I told you, I'm in this until the end. I hate the District as much as anyone."

"Not as much as me," I say.

"That may be true, but you're not a special case. The District has destroyed countless families, countless homes. I'm sick of it. I don't want to live in a world where I have to fear the zombies *and* the District."

"Lilly," I say, "it's dangerous. I don't know where I'm going. I don't know what will come of this."

"That's the point," she says. I'm surprised to see a smile on her lips. Then again, Lilly is pretty good at surprising me. "Danger is my middle name. Well, actually it's Gertrude—"

"Gertrude?"

"Don't ask," Lilly says, putting up a hand. "Anyway, I'm coming with you. You need backup, and if you say no, I'm just going to follow you."

The front door opens. I imagine it is normally soundless, but since Bandit rammed through it during his failed escape it practically screams. Suzanna comes out, a dish towel over her shoulder. For someone who has been forced to manual labor and running from zombies for however long, she seems to be adjusting quite well.

"Everything okay?" she asks.

I nod and say yes, but Lilly cuts me off as she's so apt to do and says, "No. No, it's not."

Suzanna furrows her brow and tilts her head. "What's wrong?"

"Jack here thinks he can take on the entire District by himself," Lilly answers.

Sudden anger flares inside of me. "Lilly," I say, feeling betrayed.

"Oh, stop it, Jack. We can trust her. We saw her put a bullet in Bandit's head."

"Yes, you can trust me. What is she talking about, Mr. Jupiter?" Suzanna asks me. She crosses her arms and looks at me in a very motherly way despite only being about a decade or so older.

"It's nothing, really," I say. "And just call me Jack, please."

Lilly sighs. "You're unbelievable, Jack."

Suzanna walks down the steps and comes toward us. She takes the dish towel off of her shoulder and leaves it on the railing. "You can talk to me, Jack," she says. "I know more about the District than I ever wanted to. Working here for all this time has done that for me." She puts her arm around my shoulders. In a way, she reminds me of Eve, Darlene's mother. Even up until the cancer took her, Eve had all the traits of a true leader, just as Suzanna does. She makes me feel welcome, comfortable. "Let's take a walk and discuss what's troubling you."

And what am I to do? Refuse her, run away? No, I can't do that. As much as I don't want to discuss these things with Suzanna—or anyone for that matter—I do realize that her knowledge may help me on my journey.

She leads me to the duck pond. The water is smooth, calm, and dark. The moon reflects off of its surface. Somewhere at the bottom, Bandit's body rots. He won't be coming back as a zombie, not after the shots that took him to his death landed. The image of his eviscerated face jumps into my mind. A chilling voice says *That could be you, Jack...if you don't listen, if you don't plan this right.*

I shake my head slightly in an attempt to make the voice go away. It doesn't. That voice is always there, always will be. It's the voice of doubt and fear, one that has grown from a barely audible whisper into a yell.

"We heard a voice over the radio right when Bandit ran out of the house," Lilly says.

Suzanna nods with sagely wisdom. She no longer has her arm around my shoulders; now her hands are buried deep in the pockets of her borrowed pants.

"Jack knew the voice. It's one of his old friends from Haven," Lilly says.

Suzanna pauses in her steps and looks at me curiously. "Haven?" she says.

I close my eyes and slowly nod.

"Horrific thing that happened there," Suzanna says. "But let's not harp on the past. I'll tell you what your friend is doing with the District. You may not believe me, you may not think it's the most logical answer, but I will tell you anyway."

24

The door opens back at the house, the hinges screeching. We all turn to look and there's Marco coming out on the porch with his rifle in hand.

"What's up?" Suzanna calls to him.

"Everyone's hitting the hay. I volunteered to take first watch," Marco calls back.

Suzanna wears a motherly smile on her face. She puts her hand up and says, "Nonsense, Marco. You get yourself to bed. I'll keep watch." Marco opens his mouth to protest, but Suzanna continues on. "If anything happens, I'll wake you."

Marco's mouth closes. "Of course, ma'am," he says after a moment. Then he's mumbling, barely audible, "A bed. Man, an actual bed."

The door opens again and eases closed.

Suzanna turns back to Lilly and I. "I have witnessed terrible things firsthand, as I'm sure we all have. But I've also witnessed things not even I believe."

"Like what?" Lilly asks.

"In a moment, Lilly," Suzanna says. "Come, let us go to a place more private."

She leads us to the barn. In the moonlight, the sludge-like blood from the zombies still stains the grass in patches. The air still smells like burnt meat and I imagine it will for a long time. Of all the private places on this farm, I did not think the barn would be near the top of the list, especially with Suzanna's history. She pulls up two overturned buckets for Lilly and I to sit on and then plops down herself on stacked bags of feed or fertilizer. An array of farming equipment hovers over her head—hoes, rakes, spades, all of which would be decent weapons for when the ammunition runs out.

The inside of the barn does not smell pleasant. It is a sickening sweet mixture of hay, the outdoors, and the dead. Not to mention the stink coming from the cell Suzanna and the rest of her people came from. They didn't exactly have plumbing in there.

Suzanna sighs longingly. Lilly and I exchange a glance. Worry overtakes me. Have we misjudged this woman? Has being locked in here, beaten by District soldiers, driven her mad? I sure hope not, but I clutch my rifle a little closer to my side, ready to bring it up at a moment's notice. It's now that I notice just how bare my back feels without my sword and sheath attached to it. My cloak is inside, though, that might be what's doing it. Also, it's not a particularly warm night despite the smoldering ashes of the cremation fire nearby.

"Brainwashing," Suzanna says abruptly, the maternal quality of her voice gone.

"Brainwashing?" I repeat.

Lilly laughs. It's an uncomfortable laugh.

"Yes, brainwashing. I don't know how one goes about brainwashing—it might be very easy or entirely beyond my own intellectual capabilities—but that's what the District does. They brainwash their people. If it doesn't work, then they kill them without hesitation," Suzanna says.

My mind reels. Brainwashing? Now, I've heard and read a lot of crazy things—seen even crazier things—but brainwashing? That's something else.

"I can tell by your face that you do not believe me, Jack," Suzanna says. She doesn't sound angry or disbelieving but perfectly natural instead. "I've seen it myself. These soldiers, Bandit had words for them, like dog trainers have for their dogs. He'd tell the soldier to jump and say the word and the soldier would ask how high."

"I've never heard of this," Lilly says as if her knowledge of such things is the be-all, end-all of this matter.

"Where do you come from?" Suzanna ask.

"Freeland. A sometimes District-occupied place. We supplied arms and crop for their *'protection.'* I was around District soldiers all the time, and I never heard of brainwashing—" A momentary spark of realization comes to Lilly's eyes.

Suzanna is nodding.

Me—I'm confused as hell.

"You see it now, yes?" Suzanna asks. "Now that I've pointed it out to you, you cannot unsee it."

Lilly whispers, "Holy shit. Oops, excuse me, Suze."

Suzanna waves a hand, turns to me. "And you, Jack?"

"What am I looking for?" I ask. "What am I trying to realize here?"

"Their faces," Lilly says. "Their eyes. They all look like drugged-up puppies."

"I think that has more to do with their stupidity than it does being brainwashed," I say.

Suzanna chuckles. "Relative IQ score has a lot to do with it. It's much easier to brainwash those of lesser intelligence. Those who are smart enough will just blindly follow orders for fear of their lives, but they are few and far between. The Shadow likes to keep his lackeys...*lacking.*"

"The Shadow?" I ask. Brainwashing is one thing. I mean, I've heard of brainwashing, maybe even suspected it of the District soldiers at some base level, but I've never heard of The Shadow, or anything involving shadows when it comes to the District.

Suzanna nods. "Yes, he is also known as the Overlord."

My stomach squirms. Inside of its pit is a snake of fear and loathing and anger and hate. "Also known as the one-eyed man."

"So you've seen him?" Suzanna says. "I never have. Bandit always made house calls. Slaves such as us wouldn't have seen the light of day had it been the other way around."

I try to hide the anger on my face. Always simmering just below the surface is my hatred for the one-eyed man. These days, two years after my wife and son were taken from me, I have learned to control it slightly, to bury it a little deeper. Now, though, I can feel the heat baking my face, my hands shaking, my blood pressure spiking.

"More than seen him then, hmm?" Suzanna muses. "He has wronged you personally. That is evident enough in your eyes."

I'm quiet for a moment, quiet and still, stewing in my own hatred and subtle panic. All my time on the road, I've wondered about this one-eyed man, this Overlord. I've heard a million different stories of who he is, but most of them were just that—stories. Some of the District soldiers I've come across during my travels did not even believe this Overlord existed, he was an urban legend to scare those into action as some shady government organization left over from the old days tried to put the pieces of the shattered world back together.

"He did more than wrong him," Lilly says in a low voice. I look up at her, my eyes blazing. She catches the hint. "Well...it's not my story to tell."

"Not one I feel like telling, either," I say.

"That's no problem. I understand," Suzanna says.

"What do you know about him?" I ask.

"Not much. Only what I've heard over snippets of conversation from Bandit and his men."

"I've heard a lot of bull," I say. "Why should I

believe you?" I don't mean this to sound harsh. It kind of does.

She looks at me, not in the least bit offended. "Does it matter, Jack? All you've heard may be true, it may be not, but it doesn't matter in the grand scheme. You only want one thing, I see it in your eyes as much as I see the pain and hurt in them."

I look away. I can't help myself. It's as if Suzanna isn't looking at me so much as she's looking *through* me. I feel exposed.

"I'll tell you what I know," she continues. "What I've heard."

I almost stop her, almost raise my hand and say I don't need to hear this. She's right, you know. None of this matters. The Shadow, the Overlord, or the one-eyed man. He could be Ghandi reincarnated for all I care and I'm still going to get my revenge. Because what it comes down to is the fact that he took my wife and son away from me; he slit Darlene's throat and stepped on Junior's back as he shot him in the head; he ruined my life, all that I've built up, all that I had.

"His name was Adam. He was an investment banker long ago, and those types of skills one learns in investment banking do not transition well into the zombie apocalypse. So him surviving is almost unheard of. But then something happened. The story goes he was on the run after his compound was flooded with rotters."

Lilly adds in, "A feeling we all know," as I continue to look away from Suzanna, trying to force my mind anywhere else. But I can't. I have to listen. For Darlene, for Junior, for Abby and Norm and Herb and Tim and Carmen.

Suzanna doesn't seem to notice Lilly's comment and continues talking. "It was while on the run that Adam began to be haunted by what has come to be known as The Shadow."

"Like a ghost?" Lilly says skeptically.

"Like a ghost," Suzanna agrees. "This ghost or shadow or spirit—whatever it was—made Adam do terrible things. I've heard that by this point in time he had lost his wife on the road. Those among his group were his wife's cousin and a friend from the camp they'd been driven out of. One night, Adam sat by the smoldering remains of their fire on watch. The voices inside his head were always there, I assume, but then they were so loud, he couldn't avoid them. They told him to kill his wife's cousin, to kill the friend. And he did it while they were sleeping. He took their lives for no apparent reason, and on that day a new alliance was forged between The Shadow and what was left of Adam's mind."

"What is The Shadow besides a ghost?" Lilly asks. "Like, really?"

"I—I don't know. Does it matter?" Suzanna asks. "It is evil, whatever it is."

I let out a shaky breath, tune back into the conversation.

"Holy shit," Lilly is saying. "That just sounds...crazy."

Suzanna shrugs. "It gets crazier still. This spirit so tormented Adam that he listened to its every word just to appease it. Even when The Shadow called for Adam to remove his eye. One of the men passing through Bandit's farm claimed to know the soldier who walked in on Adam doing this. He did not use anything besides his own finger, digging and digging into the soft flesh until the eyeball came out with a suctioning *pop*. The man saw his eyeball hanging from one tangled and stretched optic nerve, saw the blood cascading down his face like red tears. The floor was soaked with puke and blood and pus, and Adam turned around, not Adam any longer for the transformation had been complete that night, and shrieked at the top of his lungs for the soldier to leave or it would be his eye that was removed next."

Lilly and I look on; her shocked, me unamused. Nothing seems to shock me anymore.

"He didn't require any medical attention. It is said The Shadow healed him in a matter of days. There was no infection or complications. He did not wear an eyepatch, either," Suzanna says.

I nod, the image of the man fresh in my mind. He hadn't wore an eyepatch when he murdered Darlene and Junior. The hole was a raw mess of red and pale-white flesh, twisted and pinched to look as unnatural as Suzanna's story sounds. Thinking of that wound makes me want to scream in rage, to find him and pull his other eye out.

I push myself up from the bucket, step out of the barn and into the cool, smoky night air.

Suzanna pauses for the moment. I turn to look at her, the queasiness ramping up with the movement. "What does this have to do with Abby?" I ask.

"Everything," Suzanna says. Her face remains blank and stony. "Your friend is under the influence, to an extent, of The Shadow, and I'm afraid there is no possible way to save her. She is lost, lost forever."

Lilly hangs her head down. I don't. This is bullshit, I know it is. Abby recognized my voice. If she is brainwashed and she recognized my voice once, that means it's not too late to break that spell.

Somewhere under her trance, she is the Abby of old, the sister I've never had.

Or what if it's a setup? What if she faked it and they're waiting for me? But why would they want me? Unless…someone from Freeland helped spread my little run-in with Brandon and the other District guards to the higher-ups. Maybe the one-eyed man thought I was dead and after hearing the story he finds out he was wrong. What would be the best way to get me to him? Abby would.

But that's just…crazy. Isn't it?

I turn away from the barn now, the rifle over my shoulder, thumping me in the side. It aggravates an old injury in my ribs, one I never got properly checked out due to the collapse of civilization all those years ago.

No, forget it. Setup or not, I can un-brainwash her if I have to.

"Jack? Where are you going?" Lilly asks.

"To the Lincoln," I say. "I have to get to Chicago."

Lilly stands up now, too. "Not without me."

"Lilly, just stay. I can do this by myself."

"I know you can," Lilly says, "but you shouldn't."

Suzanna gets up jerkily, holding her lower back. Despite the pain she's obviously in, she offers a weak smile. "Jack, you really shouldn't go. Not yet, at least.

You are worn to the bone, that much is evident just by glancing at you."

I shake my head. "It doesn't matter. If what you say is true, I'll fail anyway."

"No, you may not. But you shouldn't go alone. The place they call Black Towers is dangerous, or so I've heard."

"Everywhere is dangerous now," I say. I turn my back on them, stopping at the stable. There, Bilbo stands with sleepy eyes. He perks up at the sounds of my footsteps. I resist the urge to stroke his muzzle, to get *attached*.

He snorts air softly.

From the stable I go to the ruined U-Haul truck. Lilly and Suzanna have followed me. "I'm not taking it all," I say. "Just enough to get by."

"Not even all will be enough, Jack," Suzanna says. "Please, don't go. Stay here and live in peace for the rest of your life."

I set the rifle I'm handling down on the hole-ridden metal floor. "Peace? No such thing as that anymore. They'll always come—the zombies, the District, The Shadow, doesn't matter."

"But we'll be prepared for them," Suzanna says.

"That's exactly what I thought. You want peace?

You have to make it yourself. It's what I intend to do," I say.

Suzanna nods. She sees there's no convincing me because there isn't. I'm going to the Black Towers and I'm going to save Abby, then I'm going to rip The Shadow right out of the man who was once known as Adam.

I load the trunk of the Lincoln up with three rifles, each with a different attachment, and as many boxes of ammunition as can fit. I take a crate of grenades, too. For a moment, I think Suzanna is going to protest me taking the car, but she doesn't. She doesn't want to go anywhere. She wants to stay and relax, and as nice as that might be, I just can't.

The spare tire is underneath the back bumper. The jack and the rest of the tools are in the trunk. I take them out. I've only changed a handful of tires in my lifetime, most of them being under the supervision of my brother Norm, who knows a hell of a lot more about that stuff than I do. Norm isn't here, so I have to make due.

As I jack the car up and begin to remove the blown tire, Lilly is over my shoulder. She corrects me and because of these corrections, time is saved. Though I don't show it on my face, I'm grateful for her.

We get the car back on all four shoes. A spare won't get me too far, so it's lucky I'm only going about fifty miles to Chicago. In all of this work, I didn't notice Suzanna has disappeared until she comes back with two red cans of gasoline. They slosh with each step she takes.

"I may not be able to convince you, Jack, but I can help you as much as I can. Here, take this." She hands me the containers. They are heavy, causing me to strain. It's a good feeling. The smell of gasoline brings up many buried memories, makes me think of the old world. Anytime I was with Darlene—before the world went to hell, that is—I always got out and pumped her gas for her. This smell engulfed me as I leaned up against the pump and laughed like an idiot at the smashed faces Darlene would make, pressed against the glass of the driver's side window. Damn it, I miss her so much.

Lilly takes the containers from my hand and puts them on the floor in the back seat.

"Thank you," I say to Suzanna.

She smiles and offers me her hand. I take it. "No. Thank you, Jack. Know that you are in my prayers—all of our prayers."

"Say goodbye to everyone for me," I say.

"I will," she says.

Lilly closes the door and comes around to us as Suzanna and I part. The two women hug each other, and for a slight moment I get this odd feeling of mother and daughter, like in some other timeline Lilly and Suzanna could've been related.

"Take care of that horse, too," I say. I won't call Bilbo by his name, that'll only solidify my attachment.

Suzanna nods.

I turn my back on her and the house as I head to the driver's seat of the Lincoln. Inside, I turn the key in the ignition and the engine roars to life. It's a good feeling, that power thrumming beneath my feet.

But there's another feeling I get now, too, as I adjust the rearview mirror to the proper spot. It's the feeling that I haven't seen the last of Suzanna and Bilbo or this farm at all.

I really hope that's true. I really hope they can find peace and hold on to each other when I couldn't.

25

By the time we see the Chicago skyline, the sun is starting to come up and exhaustion is taking its toll on me, which I can't let happen. Lilly offered to drive once and I immediately took her up on that offer. While she drove, I was too worried to completely relax. I managed to doze in and out of consciousness; at one point, I even had dreams. I don't remember them, but judging how I woke myself up by muttering, I imagine they weren't very good.

We're coming into the downtown area. I'm trying my best not to look around, unready for the pain of seeing my old home like this. As much as I didn't love the big city and the bright lights, Chicago beat the heck out of Woodhaven, Ohio, and I'd give anything for my life to be back to the way it was.

"One positive," Lilly says, snapping me out of my reminiscence of the past, "is that there's hardly any traffic."

I chuckle and nod ahead. "Yeah, only piled up cars." Which is kind of like traffic. Dead traffic.

We haven't seen many zombies yet, just the occasional stragglers, wasted away to practically nothing. They move sluggishly, without any purpose. As the Lincoln blares past them, I see their eyes light up and turn in our direction. Then we're gone and so are they.

The pile-up I just nodded to is worse than I originally thought. My idea was to hop the curb and drive slow on the sidewalk, but even that's looking impossible. I slow the car to a crawl and scan the streets for any way out.

"Shit, this isn't good," Lilly is saying. Out of the corner of my eye, I see her hands white-knuckle gripping her rifle.

"It's okay. Just have to turn around and find another way in."

"In where, Jack? We don't even know where these Black Towers are."

She's right, but I have a hunch where the place is

and I think Lilly does, too. The Willis Tower, also known as the Sears Tower. If ever there was a place to set up shop in Chicago, it would be that massive skyscraper. Hell, that whole area would be. If you cleared out the dead, you'd have quite the metropolis to play in, and I think the District is crazy and strong enough to do such a thing. But what does Abby have to do with it?

I put the car in reverse and turn around. The tires jump the curb, making me cringe at the idea of the spare dying on me in the process. It doesn't. Now we're traveling in the other direction of the pile-up.

Lilly lets out a sigh and eases her grip on the rifle.

"You didn't have to come," I say.

She says, "Shut up."

I do.

After a moment of slow driving, maneuvering through car wrecks and more pile-ups, Lilly speaks up again. Her voice is nervous. "So what the hell is our plan anyway?"

"To drive around until we see the Black Towers."

"Yeah, you said that already. We're pretty close, but I haven't seen a single living soul," she replies.

Of course, my plan isn't what I tell her. My plan is to just avoid the zombies long enough until the

District comes to *us*, then I'll get taken to Abby and I'll un-brainwash her and we'll live happily ever after. And I have no doubt that they already know we're here.

Simple. Easy.

Right?

A stretch of clear road opens in front of us. I take this opportunity to go a little faster. I don't know what street we're on, but we're framed by tall buildings on both sides. Traffic lights have fallen into a few of them, making long gashes in their glass surfaces. On my left is a dead body—not a zombie, but a *dead* dead body. I see it out of the corner of my eyes despite not wanting to look. It's like seeing a dog smashed in half on the road. You hate to see it, but you can't take your eyes away from it, either.

This body isn't fresh. The bones and what's left of the flesh have long since rotted away. The bloodstains on the concrete have only faded slightly.

Lilly moans low in her throat, grips her rifle again.

So far, it's the worse part of our trip to the Windy City, which is surprising in and of itself.

We come to a dead end on our right. It's a parking deck that curls around and around, a place that probably cost fifteen or twenty bucks to leave your car there for a few hours once upon a time. The only way to go is left or back the way we've came. I take a look at the gas gauge. We're floating somewhere between a quarter of a tank and empty. We have one extra can of gas in the backseat. Had to fill up about fifteen miles ago. This old Lincoln isn't the best on gas mileage, but it was all we could get—and much better than the U-Haul would've been had it not been destroyed in the massive shootout on Bandit's farm. We could fill up again, I know, but I don't really want to get out of the car yet. There could be snipers posted on the high buildings or monsters lurking in the shadows.

Really, it's the emptiness of this place that once held millions of people that gets to me...and the smell. The air is always tinged with rotting flesh. Knowing my luck, I'll stop the car and not be able to get it started again, or I'll get out and as soon as my boot hits the pavement, the dead will swarm. So I'll take my chances with the quarter tank of gas, won't fill up until I absolutely have to.

I slow down and begin to turn left.

Suddenly, Lilly lets out a low shriek, building into a full-on scream. I'm too shocked to do much of anything.

But I do manage to slam on the brakes.

26

A LONG, FOUR LANE STREET STRETCHES OUT IN FRONT of us.

"Go back!" Lilly yells. "Go!"

I'm too frozen to do much of anything besides keep my foot pressed on the brake. On this road, streetlights line each side. The bulbs are long gone, I think, but that doesn't matter. Fear is gripping me as hard as I'm gripping the steering wheel. Though I know I shouldn't let it.

Bodies dangle from these streetlights. Groups of them, four or five to each light. They dangle low, reminding me of clusters of bananas you used to see at the grocery stores next to those shiny bowl-like scales. Chains are wrapped around the heads of those bodies that still have them, others dangle by their arms or their waists, slumped over.

Dead.

Their bloody faces and clothes stand out against the gray and black backdrop of the city buildings.

Now this wouldn't be too bad, I guess, considering the things I've seen in my travels, but what gets me is the hundreds—no, *thousands*—of zombies below these dangling bodies. Almost every zombie has their hands up to the sky. They bat and swing at the low-hanging bait, apocalyptic fruit trees. The closest cluster of dead are about fifty feet from the Lincoln and when they hear the idling engine (which is entirely too loud in this quiet city) hundreds of golden eyes look in our direction.

A sudden jolt of pain in my arm. I'm dimly aware of it being Lilly's hand. She's graduated from holding her rifle to digging her fingers into my flesh. Somewhere in all of this confusion I think of getting a bruise. I hate being bruised.

"Go!" Lilly yells into my ear.

The zombies are slowly breaking away from the streetlights. Their arms come down almost one by one, like they're doing the wave at a football game. Then the Domino Effect comes into play. The closer zombies have set off a chain reaction. As this group notices us, turns around, and starts shambling toward the Lincoln, so does the group behind them, and behind them, and so on.

A sudden burning on my face. The sound of skin connecting with skin. My eyes close and for this split second that they're closed, I think everything will be gone when I open them, everything will be normal. Darlene will be back with Junior alive and smiling in her arms, the past two years will have never happened, the one-eyed man would've never attacked Haven and we'd all live happily ever after.

It's a go-to fantasy of mine, I know. I can't help it.

This isn't the case, but as I do open my eyes, I realize I'm no longer frozen. Lilly has slapped the fear and shock right out of me.

I shift into reverse and my foot jumps from the brake to the gas. The screeching of the tires drown out the guttural groans of the horde—for the most part. As I start cutting the wheel to turn around and go back the way we came, the spare gives out on us with a muted *pop*.

The car rocks back and forth and for a moment I think we're about to flip. Wouldn't that just be my fucking luck?

It doesn't happen, but I do lose control of the car. It spins out and the next thing I know the back of the car smashes into a nearby traffic light, taking out a blue USPS box in the process. Old paper flies into the air and comes down like snow.

Lilly and I fly forward. Her airbag comes out and softens her blow, but mine doesn't and the steering wheel is there to greet me. Right in the face.

The world spins, goes black for a moment, and I'm willing myself to get it together, to resist the urge to pass out or die.

Glass breaks.

Snapshots of real life come to me. Speaking of snapshots, I think I'm somehow grabbing the locket that has come out from beneath my shirt. Then my eyes flutter and it's like one of those old-time movie reels. Subliminal messages of the dead spliced into the film. Here's a woman with half of her face eaten away, moving with a useless leg dragging behind her. Here's a man with his neck broken, head dangling back and forth every time his feet touch the ground. Behind them are more. An old deteriorated fella with reading glasses hanging around his neck. A black man with a dingy gold necklace *welded* into his flesh, not dangling. Indiscernible faces of the dead. Zombies in ratty suits. Some in street clothes that have turned to rags. Greasy clumps of hair. Exposed innards. Guts hanging out of their stomachs like slimy snakes.

Then, the blackness again.

C'mon, Jack. You have to get up. You have to fight. You have to move! It's Darlene's voice, coming from somewhere deep in my subconscious.

I'm slipping.

JACK!

Slipping.

Dad. Wake up, Dad!

A new voice, the voice of my son.

"Junior," I say with a croak. Blood floods my mouth and there's a sharp pain in my forehead where the steering wheel broke my momentum—as well as my orbital bone.

Something touches my shoulder. It's cold and wet. I turn my head in the direction of the touch, somehow.

There, glowing and radiant, is Junior. He has a wide smile on his face. He looks so much like Darlene. He's got her eyes, her nose...

I smile back.

Groggily, I say, "Junior."

He opens his mouth, those grinning teeth parting. No words come out. Just a gurgle. In fact, this noise has no emotion in it whatsoever.

Then it hits me as hard as the car has hit the traffic pole behind us. That's not my son, that's a zombie.

My heart leaps in my chest. Eyes open wider than they ever have. I'm back in the now, back in the terrible now. Zombies surround the car. The windshield is cracked wider than before, a jagged lightning bolt running across its width next to the stars from Suzanna shooting at the fleeing Bandit back at the farm. Lilly's moaning. The sound is muffled. There's bright red on the powdery white of the airbag. The driver's side window has shattered, glittering shards are stuck in my cloak and embedded in my arms. The pain comes full-force now. I have to try to keep it at bay as I move my hand toward Lilly's rifle. Where mine went I have no idea, but I do know that there's a zombie sticking his moldy arms into the car, reaching for my throat.

Not even the adrenaline can keep the fire in my head from subsiding.

I grab the rifle. It feels like it weighs a million pounds, the heaviest thing I've ever lifted. Somehow, I do lift it. Maybe it's now a natural motion, something my body will never forget, like breathing or blinking. The gun comes up. I'm trying to aim it at its face, sloughed-off skin, broken teeth. Can't reach it. Not strong enough.

I pull the trigger and I lose control. The gun blasts off a succession of shots and each one lifts it higher. Blood splatters the inside of the Lincoln as this eager zombie is ripped apart. Then the next shot reaches its head. It pops with an explosion of red and black. The tang of rot and coppery blood fills the cab and my mouth.

Beside me, Lilly stirs, coming back to consciousness. The rifle's burst of shots is an alarm clock, the most effective one I've ever heard.

"We gotta go," I say. "Can you walk?"

"Oh," she moans, "I think so."

We don't have much of a choice. I throw the door open and spill onto the pavement. Shards of glass dig through my pant legs, bite into my knees. The door acts as a shield from the other zombies for a time, enough for me to limp around the other side. Their collective weight would be no match for me and as I'm almost near Lilly's door, my own door slams shut. The shield is down.

Lilly moves on her own volition...mostly. I have to help her out and it's painful. I'm biting my tongue to distract from the pain.

A zombie reaches for me, grapples the back of

my cloak. The cold chain around my neck with the picture of Darlene and Junior stretches. I spin around with almost as much speed as is normal and blast this zombie woman's face to shreds. In the process, the bullets that don't hit the mark take out three other stragglers.

I tell myself not to look up, not to see how many more are closing in on us, and let me tell you, that never works. It's like saying don't look down when you're standing on the edge of a skyscraper.

"What about the weapons?" Lilly asks.

"Leave them," I say. I push her in the direction of an alley. When I say leave the weapons, I meant the ones in the trunk. My sword is in the backseat, and I can't leave that. So I lean into the car, against my better judgment, I might add, and grab the sheathed blade. Guns run out of ammunition eventually. The sword won't.

27

By the time I reach the alleyway Lilly has disappeared to, the amplified moans reaching my ears, Lilly is already at the other end. She has stopped. She's standing there with her back bent, looking like she's in pain.

I catch up to her. I have to do my own zombie walk to make it, but I do.

She still hasn't moved. This is starting to worry me, and right now, with the wall of dead closing in on us, I don't need another worry added to my growing list of things to worry about.

"Lilly?" I say, surprised at how strong my voice sounds. I feel anything but strong right now. Luckily, I've been able to ride a wave of adrenaline, but it's already depleting.

She doesn't answer.

"I'm unarmed," she says instead, and I'm wondering who she's talking to. Can't be me.

Then I see who it is.

My zombie shuffle comes to a stop about fifteen feet from the mouth of the alley. Vision isn't what it used to be and nailing my head on the steering wheel didn't help much, but a blind person could see the men and women who crowd around Lilly. They all have guns, big rifles like the kind we stole from Paul and Duane.

"You!" a man shouts. "You stop right there!"

Now, I'm no longer the Jack Jupiter I used to be, no longer that writer turned snarky action hero, but this close to the end, able to see the light at the other side of the tunnel, I think I have to be.

So I don't stop, don't listen to this asshole. Or at least, I don't act like this is exactly what I want. Can't let them know I want to get captured and taken to Abby. I turn around. The zombies stream in the opening where the Lincoln sits, crashed and forgotten. The image that comes to mind is of sand going through an hourglass. The slow drip of an IV. They are too smashed together, too eager to get at this reachable fresh meat, that they're getting wedged between the buildings. I wonder what will give way first, the zombie's rotten bodies or the brick. You may think that's an easy question to answer, but seeing what I see, I know it's not. They're so many that the brick seems to swell until it can't hold it much longer. Then these savage beasts trample each other, tearing off rotten flesh, exposing cranberry-red innards, sending brick dust into the alley.

"Stop or I'll shoot!" the same man says.

This time, I do stop. I put my hands up and turn around slowly.

"Always gets them," this man says. He says it loud enough to be heard over the squelching and tearing and death rattling.

"Drop your weapons and come forward," a woman says. She has prematurely gray hair and a face like a weathered headstone.

I do as she says. Lilly is looking at me out of the corner of her eyes, hands still raised, nose and lips still bleeding.

I walk up next to her and the man tells me to get on my knees and hold out my hands. I do this, too, only because that moaning and rattling is weighing heavy on my shoulders. I can feel this wave of death heading for the coast, ready to drown us all.

"All right, good. I like when people listen to me. It's not often that that happens," the man is saying.

He takes handcuffs out and puts them harshly around my wrists.

"Don't you think we can do this a little farther away from the dead?" I say. I'm not trying to be sarcastic. The man doesn't like it. He snarls at me. This is a man who no longer fears the zombies, not even a horde like the one behind us.

"Idiots messed up the feeding frenzy," the woman says.

"Don't worry about it, Gina. Quincy has meat duty," the man who handcuffed me says.

"Meat duty? Hell naw, I don't got meat duty. It's your turn, Mark," this one known as Quincy says. He's a young black man with a face as hard as stone.

"I'll flip you for it."

"No, ain't no flippin when it's your turn!" Quincy yells back.

Behind us, the zombies are closer.

Closer.

Always closer.

A rising panic hits me. It's like two guys arguing on a set of train tracks while a freight barrels down on them. I have to speak up.

"Hey, can we move this along?" I say. "I don't particularly want to be something's dinner today."

"Ain't gonna matter much, man," Quincy says.

"Soon as we get back to ol' Ab, y'all's dead meat anyway."

Ab. Abby. The sound of her name is enough to vanquish any of the panic and fear that has settled in me.

"Real nice," Lilly says. "So much for manners."

This raises a laugh from both the woman and the man with the other set of cuffs. He's still chuckling as he slips them over Lilly's wrists. I notice he doesn't put them on her as tight as he did to me. Maybe he does have some manners.

"Seriously though, fellas," Gina says, "they're getting awfully close."

Now that we're both cuffed and unable to harm these District guards, Mark seems to relax a bit. He lowers his rifle, lets it hang on his shoulder, then raises his arms and shouts, "Bring those motherfuckers on! I'll kill them all."

Great, I think to myself, yet *another* psychopath to deal with.

"C'mon, Mark," Gina says, her voice matronly.

The yell dies out and now Mark grabs his gun again. "I'm sorry," he says to me.

And I look at him, confused. "For what? For doing your job—"

He raises his rifle up like a club. "For this."

28

Waking up is painful. There's a dull thudding in my head that I don't think we'll ever go away. I haven't opened my eyes yet, not fully, but I know I'm back to consciousness. I guess the best way to describe what has happened is like being under anesthesia.

I've been under once before. They put the mask on me and have me count down and I start feeling cold all over, then *boom,* next thing I know I'm waking up in a different room with a fresh cut on my leg and a pin in my foot. Except, in this case right now, I wake up with nothing but a new knot on my head and a few less brain cells.

It takes me a moment to remember what exactly happened. All I really remember was a bunch of zombies, but that's no different than much of anything in this world. There's always zombies.

Opening my eyes doesn't do much else in the way of making me comprehend what's going on. I'm in some kind of conference room with a big glass wall on the end opposite of me. From the wall, I see some of Chicago's skyline. All of the other skyscrapers, the medium-sized buildings, the dead cars which look like Matchboxes from up here. Each building, it seems, is missing pieces or has been charred by fire; each building looks at me with lifeless window-eyes. It's a lonely and cold feeling that invades me. The whole city is diseased.

No, the whole *world* is diseased.

Only when I turn my head, which results in quite a few cracks and much pain, do I remember what has happened. The reason for this is Lilly. She's sitting next to me in a cracked leather chair, something an executive of a Fortune-500 company might do business from. Funny when you think about that chair, really. How it once mattered, how it was once a sign of wealth and power and respect. Now it's used to tie up nobodies in the zombie apocalypse.

This thought doesn't help much in the way of

that cold and lonely feeling, but seeing Lilly does. A familiar face is nice even if I hardly know her.

"Lilly," I say, but it comes out like a whisper. I shake my head again. The pain hits me like a tidal wave.

Seeing her there with the blood on her face and her hands tied behind her back pisses me off. I'm pissed mostly at myself. I should have never let her come along with me. She had no reason to mess up what little life she had survived long enough to cultivate.

She flicks her eyes open. One of them is bloodshot.

"Lilly, are you okay?" I ask. It's a dumb question, really. We're obviously not all right.

"My head's a little fuzzy," she answers, "but I'm alive."

"I'm sorry," I say. The words explode from my lips.

"Don't, Jack. This is what I signed up for."

The door behind us opens. It doesn't creak; the only reason I know it's opened is because I hear footfalls on the carpet. Nice carpet, by the way. Wouldn't expect anything less in a place like this.

I close my eyes to focus on the sounds. The pain that bolts through my head is almost unbearable.

Three sets of footsteps, two sets heavy, one set agile and almost silent.

"There they are," a man says. I haven't been knocked hard enough to forget that voice. It's Mark—not such a stupid name...surprise, surprise.

"What's your name?" a woman's voice asks.

My mouth parts. Relief floods me. All the tension in my body melts away. With this voice, a thunderstorm of nostalgia rushes into my head. Life flashing before your eyes—that kind. In my mind, I see a young woman of about eighteen or nineteen. She works at a gym, a gym I was so unfortunately stuck in the night of the outbreak. This girl saved me from killing myself before the zombies made their first appearance. She helped lift a barbell off of my chest—ninety-five pounds, nothing to brag about, but I don't see the point in lying here. She helps me get back to my then-fiancé and future wife. She helps me get across the country. She helps me save the world. She helps me build a community in Golden Gate Park. She keeps my hotheaded brother in line. She finds a man who accepts her for who she is, missing hand and all. She marries him. She has years of happiness before the very guerrilla group she works for took that man away from her, destroyed all that she has built, all that *we've* built.

This is Abigail Cage, the sister I never had, part of the family I've been longing to get back to for the past two years.

Hearing her voice does so much to me. I suddenly feel tears rolling down my face, slowing at the edge of my beard, getting lost in the long—and *graying*—hairs.

"Abby," I say. My voice has never shaken so much, not since I held Darlene, my wife, my love, my soul, in my arms while her blood drained from the slash in her neck, the slash given to her by the one-eyed man.

"What is your name?" Abby asks again.

I can feel Lilly's eyes on me. The tension in the room is so heavy, I think the windows will blow open.

"Abby, it's me—it's J-Jack," I say.

The footsteps again. Light, agile, almost silent.

She comes around the side of my chair and pivots. There's a bitter chill in the rush of wind caused by the sudden movement.

Now she stands in front of me, but it's not Abby, not the Abby I remember, the Abby I love. In the span of two years, this woman has aged a decade. She is haggard, her face is twisted with evil, her eyes are full of pain. I think if I blink—if I *could* blink—

that the strings attached to her limbs would reveal themselves and there would be the one-eyed man floating above us all in the darkness, controlling those strings. The thought freezes me again. I want to shout, I want to scream.

I can't.

On her missing hand she wears a metal hook, not like something a pirate would wear, but something much more sophisticated. Her clothes are too big for her body. She has lost a lot of weight.

"Abby," I manage to say. "Abby. Don't you remember me?" There's a pleading in my voice, one I never expected to hear.

I think recognition flashes in her eyes, but it's gone as fast as it came.

"How can I remember you? I don't even know your name. So what is it? I'd like to know who I am about to execute," she says.

The coldness running through me physically hurts. Execute? No. She heard me on the radio, she recognized my voice.

The tears in my eyes continue to course downward, getting lost in my beard. The throbbing in my head has flared up to something so painful, I can hardly think, let alone speak.

"Abby, you heard me. We talked on the radio. You recognized my voice," I'm saying.

"Jack," Lilly says. "Don't." This is the thudding of the casket lid, the last nail in the coffin, the first mound of dirt thrown into your grave. She has given up.

Maybe I should, too.

No part of the old Abby is present now. She is gone, gone like Darlene and Junior and Norm.

Gone.

Suzanna was right. I should've never come. I should've lived out the rest of my miserable life in silence, stuck in the past, just waiting to die.

"Jack what," Abby asks.

Behind us, Gina and Mark are chuckling. They wait for the execution, this is nothing new to them, they've seen it before. The cat playing with the mouse before she brutally tears its insides out and leaves it on the doorstep for her master. I wonder if Abby will ship my body to the one-eyed man. I wonder if he'll look upon me and laugh.

"Jack Jupiter," I answer, sounding very far away. I've already checked out, accepted my fate.

"Well, Jack Jupiter, I'm sorry it has to end like this," Abby says.

"No—" Lilly screams. "Don't do it. Kill me first."

I look at her out of the corner of my eyes, at a loss for words. Does she...does she *care* about me?

As if reading my mind, Lilly says, "We're both screwed, yeah, I just don't want to see your head blown off," in a low voice. "Don't want that to be the *last* thing I see."

Eh, I get it.

"Shut up!" Abby shouts loud enough to cause the window to rattle. It makes me jump, and I wish I could fall inwardly on myself, vanish to nothingness, leave this all behind.

The guards are chuckling. Pieces of shit.

Abby walks closer to me, her claw-hand scratching along the table, making a terrible grating sound.

She bends down, her breath hot in my face. I almost cannot meet those eyes, those *dead* eyes.

"It'll be over before you know it," she says. "One shot in the back of the head, punishment for crossing into District territory and disturbing official District business."

Shot in the back of the head, like my own son. My breathing is almost as shaky as my body. I'm thinking of Junior, of Darlene, thinking dying won't be all bad. At least I'll get to see them again in the afterlife.

"Please," I say to Abby. "Please remember." But I know it's worthless. This empty shell of a person has made up whatever it has of its mind left. Suzanna's words come into my head, a bullet to my brain —*brainwashed*. Abby is brainwashed and I can't blame her. She is doing what she's been programmed to do.

Now Abby spins the chair around.

Lilly and I look at each other as I pass. "I'm sorry," I say.

It's all I *can* say.

She smiles. It's a sad smile, a pretty smile. Gone too fast.

Then, the unsnapping of a button, that unmistakable sound of a gun being pulled free from a holster.

The cocking of the hammer.

29

I'VE PICTURED THIS MOMENT EVER SINCE I LOST Darlene and Junior. Before I lost them, the idea of death was always on my mind, too—I mean, how could it not be when there's zombies walking around to always remind you of what death is?

In the two years since I've pictured this sweet relief, this way to get back to my wife and son and all those who I lost before I arrived in Haven and all those I lost after, it was not like this. I would never in a million years think the person who was going to do me in would be a brainwashed member of my own family.

But that's the way it is.

That's the way it has to be.

I have to accept it, like I have to accept Darlene

and Junior are gone, and Abby is brainwashed, and that I'll never see my older brother again, never find out what happened to him.

To close my eyes or to not close my eyes, that is the question. Do I want to die a coward or do I want to die looking at the grinning faces of Gina and Mark?

I'm reminded of an amusement park. I don't know why. Thought I'd have a more insightful final thought, but I can't help myself. When I was younger, Norm took me to this place called Geagua Lake in Aurora, Ohio. It's gone now, gone before the apocalypse happened.

In this place, there was one of those log rides. You sat in a long car that was made to look like a log floating in water. It pulled you up a steep hill, took you around a jerky bend—at this point, you'd feel how cold the water was, and no matter how hot the temperature had been, you'd almost always regret getting on this damn thing—then you're looking down a huge drop that ends in a pool of the same cold water at the bottom. Down you went and the nose of the log would make a huge splash as it hit. Water flew up in, what seemed like to a younger me, a tsunami wave. But the reason these grinning District soldiers remind me of that ride is because there was a bridge you could stand on just over that large pool of water the log ride ended in. There, you'd get some of the splash. The idea was you wouldn't get as much as you would've had you been on the ride. I told Norm that I didn't want to ride it. He gave me his usual, *You're a wimp, you're too chicken, blah-blah-blah* excuse, and I waited for him on the bridge with the scores of other too-chicken spectators. The splash that hit me nearly knocked me off the bridge, and it felt so nice in the hot summer weather. All while saving me a panic attack from looking down that drop from the nose of the log. So I told Norm to go on it again, I wasn't feeling well, blah-blah-blah, just so I could feel the splash again and again and again. Every summer we went to Geagua Lake, this was something I looked forward to, one of my fondest memories of childhood. It was a time when Norm and I seemed to get along back then, which was not often.

I imagine the grin on my face in those days is a lot like that of the District Soldiers. As soon as Abby's bullet enters my skull, the spray of blood and brains—*my* blood and brains—is going to drench Gina and Mark, the sick bastards, and they're going to enjoy it.

So I decide to close my eyes. What if there's

lingering brain activity once the bullet slices through my head? What if the last image my dying eyes see are these two sharks?

No, I don't want that.

With my eyes closed, I muster up a family portrait in my mind. A picnic in Haven. The sun shining, the air smelling fresh. We are gathered around a tree with bright leaves. The backdrop is a clear blue sky. There, in this portrait, is Darlene, my son, Norm, Tim, Eve, Carmen, and yes, Abby before her own mind was destroyed.

I hold this image for as long as I can. It keeps the fear away, the sadness, replaces all of it with love and nostalgia.

In this peace, I accept my fate.

30

THE GUN GOES OFF ONCE.

Twice.

I hear a scream. Is it Lilly's? It must be, I can't imagine I look too good with a bloody hole in my head.

But wait—

How can I hear a scream if I'm dead?

Unless...

My eyes shoot open. My heart is pounding fiercely, it's like a running dinosaur in my chest. *Thump-thump-thump-thump.*

What I see first is a bright streak of red against the white walls. It drips slowly, pools on the nice carpet. My eyes follow it to the floor. There, a crumpled man lies, blood coming from his head.

What the fuck? is on my lips, ready to leave my mouth when I feel a tugging at my wrist.

"Don't have much time," Abby is saying. "They'll come up and check pretty soon."

I have no idea what's going on.

My eyes flick to the other body. This one is closer to the door, hardly any blood comes from it. It's Gina. Her gray hair is unmistakable. I only mention this because I'm currently wondering if I've imagined all of it. Because this is impossible. This is unreal.

I saw Abby's eyes, saw how sinister they were. She meant business. The brainwashing was real.

Or was it?

My arms are free. I pull them up, sudden pain in my shoulder, the phantom biting of the binds on my wrist. Now, a tugging on my ankles, a tearing. I look down and see a hand and a claw working on the shiny duct tape methodically, carefully.

"Abby," I say. "Abby."

"Jack, not now. We can catch up as soon as we're out of this shit-storm," she replies from the floor. I look over to Lilly. Her mouth is hanging open. There's tears in her eyes. She thought I was dead; *I* thought I was dead. "It's gonna be hard enough to get into the garage without the whole fucking squadron breathing down our necks," Abby continues.

It's now that the crumpled body on the floor starts moving. Moaning. Gina is up on all fours. She looks back at us, a flash of hate and pain in her eyes.

"Abby!" I say.

"Shit!" Abby says.

Gina opens the door as Abby shoots.

Misses. A bullet sprays shards of wood in every direction. She aims again, but the door closes after Gina slips out into the hallway.

Abby runs past me.

It's too late. There's a painful groan, practically a scream, and then a thud on the wall out there that carries far and wide.

But not as far and wide as the sound of the alarm the dying District guard has just hit.

31

I don't let this put a damper on the fact that I'm still alive. I know my opportunities when I see them, and though my feet are not untied yet, I lean over and begin working on Lilly's bound hands.

Outside, in the hall, another shot goes off and Abby storms back into the conference room. Blood dots the flesh on her neck and chest. In her clawed hand, she holds a knife. I'm guessing she took it off of Gina, who won't be bothering us again. But the deed is done. The alarm has been raised and we're on the clock, a very short clock. Soon, a stream of guards will start pouring into the room.

Abby slices through my duct tape and then does the same on Lilly's.

"C'mon," Abby says. "I can get us out of here in no time."

I stand there on wobbly legs, smiling like a fool at her. Abby fuckin Cage. It has been too long. It's almost like staring at a ghost. I was sure she was dead, but here she is.

"Close your mouth, Jack. You look like an idiot," Abby says. "And a beard? C'mon, man, you cannot pull off a beard!"

I smile, tears in my eyes. This is a dream. It has to be. I'm imagining Abby and her voice like I've imagined Darlene's and Junior's.

She smiles back. For this moment, nothing exists but us. No alarm, no bodies on the floor, no zombies in Chicago or the world—just Abby Cage and Jack Jupiter. Reunited.

I can't help myself. I lunge forward and hug her, mostly to make sure she is real. Her warm flesh against my own says she is.

"Blah," she says. "Save the sappy shit for later... you know, like after we're dead."

"Gonna be sooner than later," Lilly says. She points to the door. Outside in the hall, the unmistakable sounds of running footsteps and confused shouting echo.

"Let's go!" Abby says. Something passes between us, a mutual understanding of mutual destruction. Part of the old gang is back. We're both a little older, a little more broken, but we know you can never be too old or too broken to fuck shit up.

32

Three steps into our flight, we realize we aren't getting out of here alive...at least not through the large double doors that lead out into the lobby. Now is a good time for action-hero Jack Jupiter to rear his ugly head, I think.

"Shit!" Lilly says. "What the hell do we do?"

Tensions are somehow running higher than before. Quickly, I scan the room for anything I can use. I've already picked up Mark's assault rifle, it's currently over my shoulder, the grip firmly in my clenched hand. Wish I had my sword. Might not do me much good in this particular situation, but the cold steel has a calming effect.

The room is pretty bare. We need something to hold the doors closed while we figure out what to do next. I reach down—maybe a belt. Fuck, I never wear belts. Too uncomfortable.

"Abby, give me your belt!" I say.

She looks at me like I'm crazy.

"Just give it to me."

"Well, if I knew it was going to be like that..." Lilly says.

We both turn to her and shout, "Shut up!"

Abby takes her belt off, hands it to me. I slide it through the door handles and tie the tightest knot I've ever tied. Again, Norm would be proud.

We are backing up toward the window as the first thud hits the doors, jolts it in the middle where the two meet. Another pummel and the hinges scream like living things.

"Now what?" Lilly asks.

"We fight," Abby says with confidence. "I've done some fucked-up things over the last couple years and nothing can atone for them, but I'm glad I'm going out on a good note. Glad I'm going out fighting."

I take her right hand with my left and I squeeze.

"And I'm glad I got to see you again," she says. This emotion stuns me. Abby has always been the last to show it. "Yeah, yeah, I'll never admit I said that."

"It's not over," I say. My back is up against the window. I turn around and look down—another mistake, never look down. We're about fifteen to twenty stories up. I'm no expert, but I think that amounts to nearly two hundred feet and that's a *long* drop.

As I turn back to the door, which is probably two good hits away from buckling in, I see something out of the corner of my eye.

My breath catches, heart skips a couple beats.

What I see is hope, and it's hope in the form of a scaffold, one of those suspended scaffolds the window washers used to use. Another minor, negative detail of the apocalypse—dirty windows. Whatever skyscraper we're in right now could use a good washing.

"Look!" I say, pointing.

Abby wastes no time in looking. Lilly, on the other hand, says, "It's a bird, it's a plane, it's—" But she's looking now, and her face goes pale beneath her mask of dried blood. "You gotta be kidding me. I'm not—"

"It's either that or we get tortured and killed by the District!" I say.

"Jack, that thing hasn't been used in fifteen years

and it's not even on our level. We'll have to jump—" Lilly is saying.

"That's a risk we're gonna have to take. I'll go first and see if I can get it any closer," I say.

"Jack, you're going to kill yourself," Lilly says.

I shrug, trying to mask the fear that is close to consuming me. As hard as I've become that fear is always there. I can't let it stay, though. I have to be the leader, I have to step up.

"Stand back," I say.

Reluctantly, Lilly and Abby do.

"Open up!" a guard yells.

"You're dead!" another echoes.

I don't bother aiming, I just pull the trigger. A burst of shots shatter the large window. The glass falls for seemingly forever. A blast of wind musses up my hair and then tries to pull us to our death with a roaring *whoosh*. We resist it as much as we can.

"Jack!" Lilly says, but I'm already on the edge of the window, crouching, ready to jump.

Don't look down don't look down don't look down
I do.

The glass is still falling. The waning sun catches on the shards as they tumble over and over. Lilly is still shouting my name, the door is still being pounded on, but I can barely hear it over the wind.

Wind. So much wind.

No more thinking, Jack. Just do it! Norm would do it. So can you.

You can do this, Jack. It's Darlene's voice and it's exactly what I need to hear right now.

I jump, and for the split second I'm suspended over thin air, over nothingness, my heart stops beating, my blood stops pumping, and my brain shorts out.

Then my hands close over steel, cold steel, and my fall is cut short. The scaffold groans under my weight. I'm screaming, or am I? Who the hell knows? Everything is lost in the wind.

Somehow, I manage to pull myself up, and as much as I just want to lie here and catch my breath or never fucking move again, I can't.

Seeing that the controls on the scaffold are rusted to the point of me not being able to press the buttons, I try anyway.

Nothing but drifting flakes of rust to show for it.

"Abby!" I shout.

A sudden queasiness stirs my guts. What if I'm too late? What if they're taken already?

But Lilly's head pokes out of the window, then Abby's right above her.

"You have to jump!" I yell, voice lost in the wind.

I see Abby and Lilly exchange a glance, worried, scared expressions on their pale faces. Words pass over Lilly's lips. I don't hear them, but I'm adept enough at lip reading that I get the gist.

Fuck it, is what she says.

And fuck it is right. Lilly springs forward. She gets good air under her and makes the jump much easier than I did. I help pull her up, putting the sudden dip on the scaffold that nearly knocked me over the edge to the back of my mind. Can't let that fear consume me.

"Wooo! Holy shit!" Lilly says.

"Come on, Ab!" I shout once Lilly is safely behind me.

Abby shakes her head. *Fuck it,* on her lips, too. She jumps. Everything moves in slow motion. She seems to float for much longer than she actually is. The metal hook sending sparkles through the air, her arms and legs swimming.

A thud.

Me screaming with joy and fear and confusion.

Abby holds on to the railing with her good right

hand while Lilly and I each have a fistful of her jacket. The seams rip. I can almost hear them.

Heaving, we pull her over.

I hug her fiercely. But during this hug, the scaffold dips a whole floor. Now we're face to face with the dirty window to the left and below the window we just came from. We have to get off this fucking thing before we fall to our death, or before the District starts picking us off with their rifles.

"Controls don't work," I say.

"Doesn't matter," Abby says, her hair blowing wildly. She points to the cables. They're fraying, twanging as each twine unravels under our combined weight and its years of neglected maintenance.

Thinking fast, I aim the gun at the window in front of us, seeing our warped reflections. It looks like I'm sticking up a grizzled old man with a graying beard and his two girl friends.

Then I pull the trigger and the reflection explodes inward.

"Go! Go!" I shout, guiding them to the open window. Upstairs, unmistakable even over the roar of the wind, are gunshots. The guards have given up on the idea of busting the door down and have shot it instead. About time.

I jump in and Abby is telling me to shoot the cables. I don't think about this, I just do it. It's only when the gun clicks after my last two rounds send the scaffold to the surface nineteen stories below that I realize what she has just done.

She's bought us time. The guards will think the scaffold gave out...with us on it. Either that or we've somehow sprouted wings and flown away. Judging by their relative slowness of shooting the door open, they won't think we've found our way back into the building. I *think*.

It's crazy enough that it might just work.

Abby leads us out of the door to an empty corridor. If any guards we're on this level, they're gone because of the blaring alarm—which still blares, by the way. I'm thankful for that because it probably has masked my gunshots.

We hit the stairs.

So many steps later, Abby leads us through another door. At this point, I'm practically gasping for air.

Lilly is doing fine, so is Abby. Old man Jack Jupiter hates cardio, even when his life depends on it. Through this door is a glass tunnel leading to an attached parking deck. A guard runs through it and toward us, and I nearly trip over my own feet. He's snarling like a rabid dog, but when he sees Abby, he stops and salutes.

"The alarm," he says with an urgency that he's trying to control.

"Prisoners have escaped on level 19," Abby says. "I'm going to cut them off on the ground. Is my truck filled up?"

The guard looks confused here. "Miss Cage," he says, "I don't—"

But Abby swings her pistol and knocks the guard out cold. She looks at me, shrugs. "Still got it," she says.

"That was...awesome!" Lilly screeches.

Smiling, Abby turns and jogs to the door the guard has just come out of. I step over the guard and follow.

In the parking deck is an array of cars. Really, all types of vehicles, and there's a pretty good chance that they all work.

Abby honks the alarm on a Ford truck. It's a mammoth, four doors and huge tires. "Say hello to Sheila."

I laugh. I can't help myself. This is madness. "Sheila like—" I begin to say, but Abby cuts me off.

"Like Norm's old Jeep," she says.

Lilly looks at us. "You guys are weird."

"Oh, you'll soon join in on the weirdness," Abby says as she opens the door. "It's inevitable." Then she motions to me. "Want to drive?"

"God, yes," I say.

"Too bad," Abby replies.

All I can do is shake my head. Maybe it's not such a good idea that I drive. Didn't work out to well for me last time I was behind the wheel.

We get in the truck and she starts it up. It purrs to life smoothly, almost soundlessly. She doesn't turn the lights off. A few others are in the garage now, getting into their own rides—armored Chryslers, trucks on tires as tall as me, vans with spikes on their bumpers—all to go catch the escaped prisoners.

Abby lets them pull out, their tires screaming on the asphalt, then she pulls forward as normal as day, as if nothing's happened.

We are back on the road. She turns right when everyone else turns left, leaving the District's Black Towers and downtown Chicago behind.

Hopefully forever.

In front of us, I see the shimmering lake, and a road of possibilities beyond.

33

"My first question," I say to Abby as we get on a stretch of open road, "is how?"

"How what?" Abby replies.

Lilly is in the backseat. She has this big, goofy smile on her face, as she should. We did just escape death three times back there. Nothing new for the old Jack Jupiter, though.

"How did you un-brainwash yourself?" Part of my mind, that old writer in me, knows Abby is smart, smart enough to not get brainwashed, but that newer Jack who's lost all hope can't believe it. I'll just have to find a middle ground.

Abby laughs.

"I was never brainwashed."

I run a hand through my beard. "Never

brainwashed." So the old Jack was right. Maybe I need to start trusting him more often.

Abby shakes her head. The truck thunders by a group of zombies, their dead heads turning in our direction. We are nearing the entrance to Highway 41. Pretty soon we'll pass Soldier Field without any traffic. Coming up on our right would be my old apartment building, Pathfinder Pointe. I try to put this to the back of my mind, to focus on Abby's story, but I can't.

I never liked Chicago, thought the big city life was too much for me—not to mention too expensive. If it wasn't for Darlene's job downtown, I would've lobbied to live somewhere in the suburbs. Maybe buy a house, white picket fence, backyard, two car garage—you know, the works. But as much as I disliked Chicago, I can't help but think of all of Darlene's stuff in that apartment, all those sweet reminders of her, all those pictures, mementos.

If I could just see it one more time—

"Jack?" Abby says. "Did you hear me? Are you all right?"

I shake my head. "No, sorry. Spaced out. Car accident before we got taken hostage."

She arches an eyebrow at me.

"I love how you say that like it's not a big deal.

Never been in a car accident in my life until I got into a vehicle with Jack behind the wheel," Lilly says.

Abby chuckles. For a second, she's the old Abby like I'm the old Jack Jupiter. Nothing has changed. Everything is good.

Except it's not. Never will be.

"I said," Abby says, "long story short, I pretended to be brainwashed. Worked my way up to the top. Couldn't let myself get killed."

"Can't beat 'em, join 'em type of thing?" I ask.

"Was at first," Abby says. "But I'll admit, Jack, I was too scared to stand up to them. They're insane."

I nod. I know all too well.

I'm looking out of the window. The apartment building is right there, tall, twenty stories, green glass shining in the sunset.

"Jack?" Lilly asks.

I can't do it. I can't drive by the old apartment and not see it, not when I'm this close. "Can you take this exit?" I ask, pointing ahead.

"Exit? Jack, you can't be serious," Abby is saying. She's slowed the truck down considerably.

"I used to live there," I say, pointing at the building. "With Darlene. That's where we lived, in those apartments."

"Jack," Abby says but I barely hear her, "I know

how you feel and all. I lost Mike, but we can't stop. Not yet. They'll be scouring the city for us. Probably have eyes on the truck right now. They're *crazy*, Jack. *Crazy*."

Lilly leans forward. Her scratched up arm rests on Abby's shoulder. In a soft voice, she says, "I know stopping is dangerous and stupid as hell, but he needs this, Abby. He needs this more than anything."

Abby sighs. I'm still gazing dreamily at the old apartment building as it slowly rolls by, out of my life forever.

Abby cuts the wheel, jerking me out of this fugue state I'm in, and then we're going down the exit ramp.

34

THE APARTMENT IS JUST HOW WE LEFT IT. FIFTEEN years ago. The smell is even the same. Faint, but there. Strawberry shampoo, vanilla-scented candles. I think there's a lingering hint of the spaghetti I cooked for Darlene in the days leading up to our departure to Woodhaven.

I'm probably just imagining all this, but still, the memories and phantoms smells are as sweet as ever.

Tears roll down my face, but I'm not sobbing. Abby and Lilly are outside of the door. The apartment is on the second floor. There was a dead guy in the stairwell. He looked vaguely familiar, but had rotted beyond certain recognition, like a neighbor or a landlord. I guess I'll never know.

Here is a picture of Darlene and I in San Francisco sitting on an end table by the floral couch. I'm holding my necklace as I look at it. The picture shows the time we visited her parents on winter break in college, when we were both starry-eyed students at Ohio State. We are posed in front of the Golden Gate Bridge. She wears sunglasses. I wear a stupid hat I thought was cool at the time and a puka shell necklace. God, I was so lame.

I swipe the dust away from the frame, and there's her beautiful smile beneath it. There's the love in my eyes, the total blissful happiness.

A tear falls on my wrist.

Here's our bedroom. My feet move, but it feels like I'm walking on clouds. Our molded sheets, the bed unmade. Here, Darlene was not a firm believer in the making of beds. I chalked it up to laziness; she said it was because no one cared if our bed was made or not. Back in Haven, she always made the bed, said it was a good thing for Junior to pick up, said he wouldn't do it unless he saw Mom and Dad doing it. Lead by example. The thought brings a grin to my face.

Then I see a smutty romance book lying face-down on the nightstand, and my grin gets wider. A muscle-chested stud stares back at me from the cover with a buxom lady clutching his arm. I pick it up. She left off on a dog-eared page 138.

In this moment, everything is in a type of stasis, everything is waiting for us to come back, and knowing that Darlene and Junior never will hits me harder than ever. A Mac trunk barreling toward my heart, plowing through it, then backing over it.

Again. And again. And again.

The tears come with a noise this time. I'm sobbing despite trying to keep control of myself.

Outside of the apartment, through the cracked door, I hear a raised voice. A spike of fear sends a chill up my spine, and my hand automatically goes to the gun hanging on my side. I lost my sword, but I'll never lose a gun for long.

The voice registers. It's Lilly.

"Are you serious?" she says. "You need to tell him this. Like right now!"

"No, I'll tell him after," Abby replies.

Footsteps. The door creaking open. More footsteps.

"Lilly, wait!" Abby is saying.

"Jack!" Lilly says. She stands in the threshold of my old bedroom, where a pile of my old dirty underwear and clothes sits in the corner by the dresser, where the bed Darlene and I once made love on sits behind me. I'm holding the picture in one hand and a smutty romance novel in the other with bleary, bloodshot eyes. I can't imagine how this looks.

But Lilly pays it no mind. She has a smile on her face and hope in her eyes.

"Jack," she says, "Abby knows where your brother is."

"What?" *My brother,* I'm thinking, *I don't have a brother.* But I'm tired, I'm heartbroken, I'm scared. It takes me a moment, but of course, I do have a brother.

"He's alive?" I say in a whisper so quiet it's barely audible.

Lilly nods.

In comes Abby. "I do know where he is, Jack," she says, "yeah. But he's brainwashed. Worse than them all."

"What do you mean?"

"He's the Overlord's right hand man," Abby says. "The Shadow's shadow."

My mouth goes dry. I'm backing up, trying to speak, but my throat seems to be swelling shut. "You mean..."

"He may not be able to come back from it," Abby says. "He may be gone for good."

I've heard that before, haven't I?

In this moment, I feel Darlene's presence. She's here with me in this room. So is Junior.

Hope, they say.

Never give up hope, Jack.

Never, Dad.

I shake my head. "No. We can save him. I know we can."

Lilly still smiles. Abby doesn't. I'll have to convince her, I know I will, and I know I *can*. Suddenly, my heart pounds, my blood pumps. I'm alive. I'm alive and I can make a difference in this world even if it is beyond repair. Just like Darlene would want me to. Just like the old Jack Jupiter thought he could.

"Ohio," I say. "We're going to Ohio."

Abby sighs. "I see there's no convincing you. Same old Jack. Never change."

I offer her a grin as I look around the room.

My time here is done. I have the picture in my hand and the locket around my neck. It was good to come home, to see all of this, but I know it doesn't matter. It won't bring Darlene or Junior back from the dead. And the more I think about it, I could leave all of this stuff—the picture, the book, the locket, everything—because I know they will be with me wherever I end up.

I raise my hand and touch my chest, right above the heart I thought died a long time ago. Darlene and Junior will always be right *here*.

I look down at the romance novel, close it, set it on the nightstand.

The story has ended for now. But I'm still chasing my happily ever after, and I won't stop until I get it.

AFTERWORD

I had to do it. Had to write another one.

Jack Jupiter's story has been a big part of my life for almost two years. I originally started his tale in the summer of 2016, but set it aside and wrote other stuff. I came back to Jack's story in the fall of 2016, finished, wrote some more, and here I am. I thought *Dead End* would be the last tale in his saga.

Turns out I was wrong—I often am.

Since the last book was published, I worked on another series. An urban fantasy with portals and other worlds, and the entire time I was writing those stories, I kept thinking about Jack Jupiter. I wondered how he would be now, what he'd been up to. How he was handling being a father and a husband and a leader. These questions weighed heavily on my mind, so much so that I had to write to find out their answers.

I hope you liked it and I hope you are all right with me continuing the story. I would understand if you weren't, if you thought *Dead End* was a perfect sendoff for Jack and the gang, but, like in real life, the story isn't over until we're dead.

And Jack's got a lot of life left in him yet.

F.M.

February 4th, 2018

PREVIEW: DEAD JUDGMENT

Copyright © 2018 by Flint Maxwell

Chapter 1-

Rewind a month ago and ask me if this is how I'd expect the day to go.

My answer: It's not.

But life is full of surprises, isn't it?

I'm walking down a hill with a flare in my hand—a *lit* flare in my hand. Behind me, a swarm of the dead follow. The sight of fresh meat reinvigorates them.

I agreed because we need gasoline, otherwise our trip was going to be cut very short. I'm somewhere in Indiana, near the Illinois border.

That's how far we got before Abby's truck started to warn us that we'd be walking soon if we didn't find a Speedway to fill up at.

The problem? There's no Speedways anymore. No Circle Ks, no BPs—none of that stuff.

Luckily for us, Abby had joined a murderous cult called the District and they have their own gas operations going on in nearly every state on the east coast. I felt like dying when Abby told us this. Nearly every state? The whole east coast? The District is much bigger than I thought.

Now we're outside of one of these operations. It's dusk, the soon-to-be-winter sun sinks behind leafless trees. A chill in the air prickles my skin... well, that or the fact I'm currently shepherding a horde of zombies to the front gates of this place.

Talk about a suicide mission.

Oh well. It's all in the name of revenge.

I walk backwards now, the flare held low so the lead zombies can see it. Get them going and the rest usually follow. I can't risk thrusting the flare above my head and getting spotted by District snipers, shot dead before I'm even a hundred feet from the gate. That is if they haven't seen me already. No shots yet though, so maybe not.

Lilly charts my progress from the tree line with

the scope of her rifle. Abby is in the truck a ways off the entrance of the place. As soon as I'm close enough—

The truck revs to life and now the plan is really in motion. There's no going back now.

"Shit," I mumble and nearly trip over my own feet. If I did, the zombies would've been all over me. I catch myself and turn toward the gate. I'm running now. The truck blasts by me, a burst of cold wind blowing my too-long hair from my brow. Abby's ride is a behemoth, one of those Ford F-150s they used to advertise nonstop during football games and the like, the kind that could tow a hundred dead elephants and still somehow get thirty miles to the gallon. The gates are thick metal, but that's not a problem for Abby's truck. It plows through them, ripping them off their hinges with a shriek of steel.

I'm grateful for this because the zombies turn their attention to the chaos ensuing behind me. Voices shout from inside the gates. I think I hear a gunshot. Can't be sure, though, there's too much going on.

This is my cue.

"Hey, assholes!" I shout at the zombies. "Hey!"

Slowly, their heads turn in my direction. Yellow eyes glow in the darkness and in these yellow eyes, I see hate and pain and hunger. It's my worst nightmare. Every day in this apocalypse is my worst nightmare.

"Go get it!" I throw the flare into the compound and run away from the horde. As I'm running, of course I trip and as I trip, a straying zombie thinks I look mighty delicious. Maybe this one has evolved beyond falling for cheap tricks such as the old flare routine. I don't know. All I do know is that he's on me quicker than a dead bastard like himself has any right to be. I kick upward, hit him in the soft belly with the sole of my boot. The flesh there squishes and threatens to pop. I really don't feel like finishing this mission in a pair of gut-soaked socks so I decide my best course of action is to draw my revolver. As I do this, gunshots burst to my left. Bullets take the zombie in the head, sending a spray of brains to my right. He drops dead, his skull mutilated.

I raise my hand to the trees, toward Lilly's vantage point. "Thank you!" I shout.

Then I'm scrambling up and following the rest of the zombies into the compound.

It's chaos inside. Men and women are running from their posts, guns in their hands. It's amazing what fifty or so zombies will do to a group of people.

Dust kicks up on the path ahead. That'll be Abby's truck.

I take cover behind the thick support beams of a nearby watchtower as gunfire erupts, going off like bombs. A man falls near the opposite tower and screams as a zombie pins him down. His throat is ripped away in meaty shreds. Another zombie sees this opportunity of flesh and doesn't hesitate. Soon, five or so of the dead bastards are feasting on this District soldier. I can't see it so much as I hear it. The gush of blood, the ripping of hair, the cracking of bones. Now the silence of death.

I shake the queasy feeling from my gut. It's not an easy task. I have to move; if I don't move soon, Abby will be pinned down.

Who am I kidding? Abby can handle herself.

I spin out from the shadows of the watchtower and scan the camp. Large drilling rigs are set up all around this fenced-in piece of land. I wonder if the District knows what they're doing when it comes to drilling for gas. Doubt it. The groundwater around here is probably so contaminated from their ignorance. But I guess it doesn't matter as long as they get what they need. There's not many people left to drink the water anyway.

Past the drills is a long building. A few guards are

fighting off the oncoming wave of zombies there. This is where the gas is kept, Abby told me.

I make my move toward it, running fast, keeping my head down. I'm maneuvering through the battlefield, just waiting to be shot down.

As I approach the building, I catch the faint whiff of gasoline. It reminds me of the old world, of filling up at the local station, and this faint smell brings on a strong sense of nostalgia.

Then a guy's getting his scalp chewed off and that about slaps me in the face and reminds me that shit *has* changed.

Shit has changed *a lot*.

ABOUT THE AUTHOR

Flint Maxwell lives in Ohio, where the skies are always gray and the sports teams are consistently disappointing. He loves *Star Wars*, basketball, Stephen King novels, and almost anything falling under the genre umbrella of horror. You can probably find him hanging out with one (or *all*) of his five household pets when he's not writing, reading, or watching Netflix.

ALSO BY FLINT MAXWELL

Jack Zombie Series

Dead Haven (Book 1)

Dead Hope (Book 2)

Dead Nation (Book 3)

Dead Coast (Book 4)

Dead End (Book 5)

Dead Lost (Book 6)

The Midwest Magic Chronicles

The Midwest Witch (Book #1)

The Midwest Wanderer (Book #2)

The Midwest Whisperer (Book #3)

The Midwest War (Book #4)

Something Dark: Horror Stories

Let Us Out: A Supernatural Horror Novella

Made in the USA
Lexington, KY
27 September 2018